Heidi Fausch-Pfister
Music Therapy and Psychodr.

Heidi Fausch-Pfister

Music Therapy and Psychodrama

The benefits of integrating the two methods

zeitpunkt musik
Reichert Verlag Wiesbaden 2012

Bibliographic information published by The Deutsche Nationalbibliothek

The Deutsche Nationalbibliothek lists this publication in the Deutsche Nationalbibliografie;
detailed bibliographic data are available in the Internet at
http://dnb.d-nb.de

Printed on acid free paper archival quality

Introduction

That which emerges from the sea of the unconscious through music therapy, can be pulled ashore by psychodrama elements.

This is not surprising, since for centuries, music and drama have been artistically combined, and today's innovative technologies make this combination more effective than ever. Images and words tell a story and music amplifies emotions. Modern media such as films and musicals address all layers of society. Hardly anyone escapes the effects of these media. Similarly, music therapy and psychodrama are suitable for many people, regardless of education, age or talent. Music is an art form that exists in every culture, and has been used therapeutically for centuries. Many different types of therapeutic approaches have developed all over the world. In the 20th century "psychodynamically oriented music therapy"was developed. I rely on this eclectic approach, which is a part of my own training and is the official school of thought in Europe today. I began my therapeutic studies at the C. G. Jung Institute with an emphasis on symbol and dream work, association and imagination; afterwards I trained as a music therapist and then as a psychodrama therapist.

When certain psychotherapeutic methods are chosen in music therapy, the goal is to optimize and enhance processes, and to sustain the effect of the therapy results. Optimization succeeds particularly well when the therapeutic journey takes place on different levels, with different media. Equally useful for the patient is the conscious understanding of the process and the ability to remember it in order to bridge therapy with daily life. This is precisely where psychodramatic techniques and tools are very useful. They act to support the focus on topics and to intensify and structure the transfer of learned material to daily life and of problems to therapy. Connecting these two art therapies is also suitable in part for use in counseling, education and supervision.

Moreno (1999) called his discovery a "three-part action method: psychodrama, sociometry and group therapy". Participants are asked to get into the action, as in active music therapy. In both methods the patient should first experience him or herself acting according to his own journey plans. Beyond the methodology, the therapist is expected to support the development of the patient's self-responsibility.

Regarding the content of this book, the aim of the text is to carefully observe the effects which music therapy and psychodrama elements produce and what their functions are. The most important functions are summarized in the table, "Psychodrama Elements with their Functions and Effects" at the end of Chapter 4. Subsequent chapters present the most frequently used elements of music therapy. Their integration in music therapy is documented with examples from practice and supplemented with suggestions for forms of play. These should stimulate implementation and illustrate what is important when choosing the best plays from our "treasure chest".

One could argue that this book describes psychodrama rather than music therapy. This is correct to the extent that the effect of music is not analyzed further, since that would extend beyond the scope of this book. For these questions I refer the reader to the vast new literature on music therapy research. The focus here is the application of psychodrama elements in music therapy. Since these elements are examined in detail, it may also benefit psychodramatists.

Music therapy and psychodrama are both comprehensive psychodynamic procedures, each requiring four years of intensive training. Nevertheless, I hope to stimulate the interest of colleagues in different therapeutic areas in the combination of the two methods and their potential applications.

1 Music Therapy, an Integrative Procedure

Whether engaged in actively or passively (receptively), music therapy creates closeness and intimacy between patient and therapist, which allows the exploration of the subconscious and facilitates the establishment of a relationship. As a consequence, deep changes become possible.

Unlike other forms of therapy, music therapy has roots that are thousands of years old and has neither an inventor nor founder. The common factor in all forms of music therapy is the use of music. Throughout the world, music therapists have developed unique methods for their fields of application based on their own cultural backgrounds.

1.1 Music, the Central Medium in Music Therapy

The beginnings of music go back to the time of Cro-Magnon man in the Stone Age. Flutes made of bone have been found dating from this period. Marcel Dobberstein (2000) believes that it is no coincidence that a jump in human evolution coincides with the emergence of music. He suggests that the arts, especially music, have an existential meaning and function, and that from an anthropological view, music is instinct-reducing, allowing man to act as a free being. In his view, the direct action of music on the limbic system and on underlying processing areas of the brain produces strong emotions, allowing music to create free space for these changes:

- In experimental acting, music can elicit creative methods of survival and allow personal expression.

- Singing and making music together allow self-expression and participation as well as the feeling of belonging to a group.

- Group singing allows the development of a group identity. Ordinary practice develops into something with rules/laws, and this promotes socialization.

- Music is always in the moment, as fleeting as time. It has structure, form and "sound material", and yet is intangible. Aside from musical instruments, it leaves no traces. The first documentations of music describe the activities surrounding the making of music, but not the music itself.

- Music is created by repetition and variation. The expectation of a customary course of the music (the result of learned probability) characterizes folk music to this day.

Even today, folk music groups, clubs, cultures and subcultures have "their" music with specific sound material for their socio-cultural expression, which forms a kind of social code. In times before musical notation these characteristics were likely to be more crucial. Court music, church music, and country music were distinguished in Europe through audio material and the instruments used. Churches and political regimes discouraged free musical styles for good reasons, since having one's own music and songs strengthens self-determination.

Revolutions had their songs. Young people often try to distinguish themselves from the older generation with their music. The influence of music on man is undeniable, especially in paving the way for new developments. This quality of music is utilized in music therapy.

Since music activates several areas of the brain (Spitzer 2003), it can lead to new neuronal connections. Simultaneous visual, aural, emotional, and kinetic (moving to music) stimulation, enables new experiences.

Sandra Lutz Hochreutener (2009) distinguishes two directions the effect of music takes, impression and expression.

Impression involves:
–   Basal stimulation
–   Cognitive stimulation
–   Spiritual stimulation
–   Activation
–   Calming effect
–   Deep relaxation
–   Structuring/patterning
–   Holding (the sense of being safe)
–   Associations
–   Intensification of experiences
–   Integration

Expression involves:
–   Container function (music as a receptacle in which feelings may flow freely)
–   Creation of Symbols
–   Sensomotoric conflict
–   Vehicle function (music as carrier of feelings enabling the expression of unspeakable things)
–   Catalyst function (reinforcement of feelings)
–   Self-empowerment (the instrument strengthens our means of expression)
–   Protection (the sound in the room as well as the instrument itself can protect, e. g., from fear and resistance).

Studies on the effects of music continue. A couple of references from professional literature are Isabelle Frohne-Hagemann, who discussed the effect of music with respect to diagnosis (1993), and Fritz Hegi and Maja Rüdisüli, who have written about their research results regarding musical components (2011).

The style of individual pieces of music, sounds and melodies, acts in different ways on people. In therapy we observe reactions and investigate the musical biography. Bell sounds from churches or cow bells, Christmas songs, national anthems, church hymns, children's songs and other pieces of music, noises and sounds may produce deep feelings of security or danger, depending on what past episodes or feelings are elicited. For example, the sound of a monochord or polychord can have a strong calming and relaxing effect, but can also have a threatening effect. I experienced the latter with two groups of people of different biographical backgrounds, first with individuals who had experienced military air attacks in shelters and secondly with individuals whose mothers suffered from severe depression during pregnancy. In these individuals the polychord sound provoked a crisis (panic, shortness of breath, palpitations, crying spells). Other biographical events can result in unusual reactions to a piece of music (see "Example from practice: Mental warm-up by a member of a music therapy encounter group", Ch. 6.2).

Marcel Dobberstein (2000) has noted that with such experiences it is less the form of the music that causes the feelings, than the memories and habits connected to it. This is in accordance with my experience. Dobberstein also proposes that the wish for perfection and playing music from sheet music act through a cognitive mode instead of an emotional mode. He notes that with the demands for perfection or the reading of music we have to think, and feelings move more into the background. Here Dobberstein also sees the possibility that the experience in the emotional mode is perpetuated, and since it refers to a past experience, is very intense. The freer mode of thinking allows for more variations and new creations, but this mode is also more distanced. Dobberstein refers to music in daily life, but his observations hold true for the music therapy setting as well. Even the handling of unusual new instruments which force us to think, can keep us in a reflective mode, yet can also playfully stimulate new creations and the overcoming of boundaries and fears.

Music therapy differs from other art therapies because of its use of musical instruments. Instruments have a strong appeal, evoking curiosity and the urge to touch them and produce sounds. Mainly instruments that are easy to play are used in music therapy. In addition, all the classical orchestra instruments plus instruments developed specifically for therapy are used, depending on the patient and the work area.

Each instrument offers different ways of playing and different functions. The sounds that can be produced with an instrument vary, too. The harmonic spectrum determines the sound quality and expression, and influences feelings. Sound intensity and resonance also vary from instrument to instrument and have different effects on the player and listener. The manner of playing has different effects as well. Whether an instrument is plucked, bowed, blown, beaten, turned, pulled, pushed or shaken, music is created through motion. This movement shapes the music in rhythm, tone color, melody, and dynamic. The player gets an immediate response from his movements. Certain instruments are very sensitive, others less so, but they all influence the player with their sonic response. They often stimulate and encourage the desire to experiment with an additional beat, to play louder, blow harder, or to create very delicate sounds. Violent youths often find a path from fixed aggressive behavior to delicate, erotic playing. Repressed feelings can be called to the surface by instruments. Music is always emotional but is unburdened by moral taboos.

The position one assumes with an instrument also influences the playing. A flute placed at one's lips and which can be carried in a coat pocket and played standing or walking, gives the player a different feeling than sitting at a piano. To hold a violin means standing or sitting facing an audience. A cello in front of the body gives a sense of protection. Playing a trumpet or a trombone can induce a sense of power and a desire to blare and broadcast something to the audience, or it can create a fear of being too loud. Sitting behind a drum armed with two sticks can give a sense of security and power. Thus the nature of the instrument and the various ways of playing it can entice players to new and sophisticated levels of self expression and self-awareness. Instruments can provide the necessary support or "cover" to encourage inexperienced singers to risk using their own voice.

Shape and materials (hide, brass, wood) also influence players. Instruments carry symbolic meanings through their shapes and uses in different cultures. For example, flutes, alphorns, and other long wind instruments are considered phallic symbols. Cellos, basses, and guitars with their curves and soft sounds are seen as symbols of femininity. Idioms also point to the symbolic character of certain instruments: "to beat your own drum" or "toot your own horn" for promoting your achievements, "bang the drum" to gather support, or "to play second fiddle" for being in a lower position than somebody else. To be in tune or out of tune, "fine tuning" (i. e., perfecting a task) or "striking a chord" are also expressions that come from the world of music.

The use of instruments in certain cultural settings influences their symbolic meaning. Is an instrument used in sacred rituals, for folk music or for the concert stage? Trumpets and harps have been placed into the hands of angels. Alphorns, which are played in the evening on the Alps, evoke peacefulness, freedom and mountain air. Soprano recorders are considered children's instruments (unfortunately) because they are often used in schools for the first music lessons.

Ultimately it is the patient who decides about the meaning a certain instrument has for him or her based on his or her own personal experience and whether it stimulates inner roles. Because of their multiple meanings and functions, musical instruments are particularly well suited as role bearers in psychodramatic interventions.

1.2 Music Therapy, from Diversity to Independent Discipline

Out of the worldwide abundance of music therapies and through international collaboration, a university subject/major emerged in the mid-20th century, resulting in a rather unanimous school of thought. *"The invention of music therapy as an academic discipline [......] which took place worldwide essentially in the 70s, had been implemented already as a merger of different psychotherapeutic directions and concepts on the background of the humanistic character of the discourse at the time."* (Jungaberle 2004, p. 15).

Research results in other disciplines, especially in neurology with imaging technology and empirical research in developmental psychology and psychotherapy, have supported the development of music therapy. Many questions about the effects of music therapy have found new answers. Research on the effect of music has been expanded by new findings in neuroscience. Manfred Spitzer (2003) for example, describes highly complex connections between areas of the brain while making and listening to music. He studied intrauterine responses to music and memories of melodies from the prenatal period. He also describes neurologic development during certain actions (Spitzer 2004). He claims that successful voluntary action in response to something new and unexpected causes an increased release of neurotransmitters. This then strengthens the neural connections of the successful action patterns and allows the re-learning of old patterns.

Music, and especially improvisation, is well suited to development of the feeling of being responsible for an action. Music provokes free, voluntary actions and the player feels responsible for each sound that his motions produce. Through the successfully produced sound he is instantly stimulated to produce more sounds.

Daniel Stern (2000, 2007) describes the developmental psychology aspect of this chain reaction and its importance for self-awareness the most important aspect being that a person can feel himself at the origin of his action. In his view, control of the action is less important than a person's need to feel like the originator of the action. This is the beginning of self-awareness. He then clearly feels himself to be the originator, especially when he receives feedback from a caring person.

In many cases it is precisely here that musical instruments with their sound echoing to the player, combined with careful musical or other feedback from a therapist, are indispensable.

Gerald Hüther (2004) addresses different aspects of neurologicy research and comes to this conclusion (translated from German): "Harmonization and synchronization of neuronal activity patterns generated in different areas of the brain are reached by listening to pleasant music, by active, playful music making, by freely singing." He notes that this harmonization results in the rebuilding of functions of the autonomic and endocrine as well as the immune system, which have been disrupted by tension, anxiety and stress. These effects have been known for a long time, but may now be demonstrated with imaging techniques.

Developmental psychology, especially infant research (Stern 2000, 2007), the discovery of mirror neurons and their psychological functions (e. g. Bauer 2006), and the discovery of lifelong neuronal plasticity, are influencing music therapy. A new understanding of the phenomena of resonance and their therapeutic importance has emerged (Gindl 2002) based on the fact that development takes place in relation to events.

The influence of musical elements in early childhood communication was shown by Mechthild Papoušek (1994) in *"Vom ersten Schrei zum ersten Wort"* ("From the First Scream to the First Word"). She claims that since early communication between parent and child is musical, it plays an important role in music therapy. Monika Noecker (1995) developed music therapy methods for premature infants. Karin Schumacher and Claudine Calvet (1999) developed a music therapy examination method based on developmental psychology, consisting of the assessment tool called EBQ (*"Einschätzung der Beziehungsqualität"*, meaning "assessment of relationship quality"), in order to document the effect of music therapy and also to have a diagnostic instrument based on developmental psychology.

Fritz Hegi (1998) developed the theory of *"Wirkungen der Komponenten von Musik"* (The Effects of Music Components). He distinguishes between five components: that sound incomprehensibly fills space and connects with the emotional world; that rhythm connects with bio- and life-rhythms; that melody combines with memories and stories; that dynamics, the polar components between loud and soft, fast and slow, tension and relaxation, relate to relationship dynamics; and that the musical form is the component that encompasses transformation and discovery. Through creative and playful rearranging of form during improvisation, new life patterns are created (Hegi, Rüdisüli 2011). In connection with the research background of psychodrama, new aspects of music therapy are emerging (see "Moreno's Role Categories" Ch. 2.3).

In view of new research results over the last decades, an increasingly unified, science based consensus from various music therapy schools (Decker-Voigt 2001) has developed through international collaboration among training programs and professional associations. As a result, music therapy may be viewed as a separate therapeutic discipline, which has music as its diagnostic and indication-specific instrument of choice (Hegi-Portmann, Lutz Hochreutner & Rüdisüli-Voerkel 2006).

In the course of this development, aspects from different directions of psychotherapy have been integrated with a sense of a "pragmatic eclecticism" (Timmermann 2004, p. 11) into the new discipline of music therapy. This is always in connection with specific characteristics of the medium of music (Decker-Voigt 2001; Hegi-Portmann, Lutz Hochreutener & Rüdisüli-Voerkel 2006, p. 13). In addition, techniques from psychodrama have also been adopted.

1.3 Music Therapy Elements Borrowed from Psychodrama

Music therapy literature often describes scene playing, role playing and various forms of stage setting as "specific" methods of music therapy. These methods all originated in psychodrama and will be examined in depth in this book.

Scene building in music therapy

Scene building found its way and became integrated into music therapy via systemic psychology. Music therapy is particularly well suited for different types of constellations, e. g., the family sculpture, since in music both synchrony and polyphony are possible. The theory and methodology of systemic work and of the multi-generational perspective in family therapy lead back to psychodrama. Psychodrama considers man as a social being (see 2.1 What is Psychodrama?) Moreno developed tools and techniques which were adopted by systemic therapists. However, psychodrama goes beyond the primary goal of systemic therapy. In psychodrama, the discussion is not only about understanding and changing social relationships, but also that individual issues, inner conditions and unconscious actions may be playfully experienced with all our senses with the goal of reviving old resources and stimulating new experiences.

In scene planning, for example, psychodrama does not limit itself to the position, line of vision and observations of the participants. The actors receive information and are introduced to their roles. The resulting play is useful in freeing blocked energy and stimulating spontaneity and creativity. More on this in Ch. 8 – Scene setting in Music Therapy and Ch. 9 – Scene change in Music Therapy.

Psychodrama not only offers additional techniques, but the effect of each technique has been and is still being studied thoroughly. These are not yet reflected in music therapy to date.

Timmermann describes music therapy scene setting in *"Klingende Systeme"* ("Sounding Systems") and mentions the special characteristics of music therapy, "like another world beyond language" (*"Jenseits von Sprache"*), "improvisation as access to the soul" (*"Improvisation als Zugang zur Seele"*), "Instruments as symbolic objects" (*"Instrumente als Objekt-Symbole"*) and "sound producers" (*"Klangerzeuger"*). He writes that a "sound atmosphere with audible symbolism" (*"Klangatmosphäre mit hörbarer Symbolik"*) is created. The practical work of setting the scene is described in terms of music therapy without specifically naming the interventions and their effects.

Barbara Dettmer (2004) describes family sculpture in music therapy. These sculptures are impressively presented, but without addressing the effect of the individual interventions. She also describes detailed responses in the direction of sharing and feedback. Psychodramatic elements are used intuitively without clearly naming them.

In "Systemic Concepts for Music Therapy" ("*Systemische Konzepte für die Musik-therapie*") (Zeuch, Hänsel and Jungaberle 2004) one finds a detailed representation of the integration of systemic concepts in music therapy, but without attention to the specific meaning of the elements borrowed from psychodrama.

Scene playing and the handling of roles in music therapy

In the current German music therapy literature, allusions are made to role playing scenes in music therapy. Christine Plahl and Hedwig Koch-Temming (2005, p. 187) mention that roles provide protection and that role playing is mainly a measure of support in pedagogy and in therapy for mentally disturbed individuals. Isabelle Frohne-Hagemann's (2005) findings are more consistent with my experience. She states that role playing provides an opportunity to assess whether the interpersonal relationship between child and therapist has been successful enough to allow therapy on a level where musical instruments can be used as role players.

Imagination, the ability to play someone else, to see musical instruments as role players and to play them, are conditions that are often absent in mentally impaired individuals. Hannelore Guth (2005) gives a moving description of musical role playing in her therapies without going into the specific results of the intervention. In an aside by H.-J. Oeltze (1997, p. 126) on role playing is a reference to the diversity of roles, and a brief remark on the flexibility of roles in the aged, but this is not analyzed further. In "Play-Music Therapy" ("Spiel-Musik-Therapie") (2009) Sandra Lutz takes a closer look at the effects of music in role playing and describes in detail role-specific intervention techniques and how they can be applied in music therapy. She refers to, among others, the psychoanalytic-psychodramatic background of Didier Anzieu (1984), who, as a psychoanalyst described psychodrama in psychoanalysis and analytic psychodrama with children and adolescents in detail; as well as to the work of H. Fausch (1998) "Music in Psychodrama" ("Musik im Psychodrama", unpublished, Thesis at Moreno Institute, Überlingen).

My goal is, among other things, to demonstrate the effects and functions of further interventions, using role playing beyond the way it is practiced today. With analysis and theoretical illumination of this background, and deliberate connection with musical and music therapeutic means, role work can be utilized even more effectively.

An overview of music therapy literature shows that psychodramatic elements are often used intuitively in music therapy, and with good results. However, the possibilities of borrowing from psychodrama are far from exhausted. Further elements may be integrated beneficially if psychodrama research is taken into account. In the following chapters the aim is to present a number of psychodrama elements in light of their function and effect on music therapy and to describe their application in more detail.

2 What is Psychodrama?

The following paragraphs describe the origin and application of psychodrama and Moreno's anthropological view of man. Music therapy and themes relevant to method integration such as tele, roles, and role categories will be discussed next. This will be followed by the introduction of terms such as stage, protagonist, warm-up, change of scene, doubling, exchange of roles, role reversal, sharing, feedback, processing, improvisation, conserve, sociometry, the social atom, and the cultural atom.

The Viennese physician and sociologist Jakob Levy Moreno (1889–1974) developed a sociology- and depth psychology-based three-part (triadic) action method: psychodrama, sociometry, and group psychotherapy. This triad is now simply called psychodrama and has been further researched and developed throughout the world.

Psychodrama can be used effectively for both ill and healthy individuals. Particularly for improving social competence, psychodrama is widely appreciated. Methods of psychodrama which have been developed further are used in therapy, diagnostics, prevention, supervision, and in the conveying of new subjects. Psychodrama is also applied in health services, pedagogy, and organizational counseling and is recognized in Switzerland, among other countries, as a method for psychotherapy (Swiss Charta for Psychotherapy).

2.1 Social, Creative, and Spontaneous

Moreno's anthropological view of man

Moreno saw man as a social creature. His interest was mainly in relationships and community. He viewed individuals as beings who exist through relationships and social roles. He saw personal identity as consisting of spirituality, individuality, and social elements. Today this view of man is found in all contemporary forms of therapy which incorporate systemic aspects, including music therapy.

Since Moreno crystallized his psychodrama elements from functions in personal interactions, it is not surprising that these elements are also part of other therapeutic methods. In music therapy they are usually used spontaneously, without being named, and their effects are given less attention than the musical effects.

For Moreno, creativity and spontaneity are central. These concepts are also central in today's music therapy. Moreno attributes a large part of human psycho- and socio-pathology to a deficient development or inhibition of spontaneity. "The central action and shaping paradigm of psychodrama is satisfied by the synergy of spontaneity and creativity. Spontaneity is most tightly connected with the psychodramatic concept of health, and impairment of the access to spontaneity is identical to the impairment of well-being and social competence" (Burmeister 1997, p. 2). Creative action arises, according to Moreno, from creativity and spontaneity and is an important condition for the shaping of personal interactions and encounters in one's surroundings. The terms "tele" and "roles and role categories" are unique to psychodrama and warrant further explanation.

2.2 "Tele", "Tele Process" and "Tele Relationship"

"Tele" is a central concept in psychodrama. "Tele", in Greek meaning "distant", "feeling into the distance" means "an instant identification with the personality of the other person and his/her mood" (Leutz 1986, p. 21). The term tele for this basic ability of man has failed to get established outside of psychodrama.

Tele is used for various phenomena in psychodrama which enable people to understand emotions, going beyond just imagining to being able to feel. Moreno did not know about mirror neurons, but he assumed their existence based on his observations. Since the discovery of mirror neurons, this human ability and ability of other species has been studied intensively and can in part be demonstrated.

"As has been shown, mirror neurons are part of the neurobiological system which mediates these exchange and resonance pathways" (Bauer 2006, p. 17). Even if fewer functions are attributed to mirror neurons today compared to when they were first discovered, they nevertheless point to a simultaneous internal understanding of perceptions, as Moreno had observed.

Moreno was convinced that *tele* was the mutual, fully developed, healthy mode of human interaction. In his view the absence of *tele* caused illness (Leutz 1986). Bauer (2006) calls the phenomenon "mirroring" and describes negative effects of absebce of mirroring on health. He claims that in the absence of this intuitive empathy, the individual drops out of the inter-personal resonance space. S/he feels surrounded by a wall of ice. Neurological changes in the brain of affected individuals can be shown. Bauer further mentions an experiment by Naomi Eisenberger who describes biological effects resulting from isolation: The pain center of experimental subjects is activated (as measured by fMRI) when they are suddenly deprived of balls by a simulated partner in a computer ballgame. The result is not surprising since today we recognize the health consequences of the absence of mirroring, be it deficient resonance in infants, bullying, or other forms of social isolation.

Moreno did not clearly delineate the concept of *tele* and used it simply to describe the mutually adequate awareness in healthy relationships as well as for resonance phenomena which are responsible for interaction in relationships and for group coherence. Sometimes *tele* stands for the tele process or for *tele relationship* (Leutz 1986).

Reinhard Krüger, a German psychiatrist and psychodramatist, adopts Moreno's way of distinguishing between tele process and tele relationship and describes the tele process in four steps, namely attraction, encounter, integration and mutual relationship building (1997). When examining a faltering/stagnant therapeutic process in light of these four steps, one can often recognize where patients are "stuck" and then continue with targeted work. For this reason I would like to describe the individual steps:

1. Attraction: To attentively notice one another. It may be neutral, friendly, or hostile.

2. Encounter: Meeting of two or more people with empathy and transference based on known experiences. This does not have to be well-meaning. Moreno explains clearly that a hostile, threatening confrontation or meeting can also be tele. The important aspect according to him is that the tele transference is reality based which is also called "adequate" (Leutz 1986). The meaning here is a perception which is not based on unrealistic transference, but on the "expected band width" as it was called by Bauer (2006, p. 26). Leutz (1986) believes that in social interactions a "negative" tele relationship (rejection) can have a more favorable effect than a positive transference-countertransference in which a mutual choice takes place, but where the partners do not connect because of the unreal transference relationship. For example, the admiring patient and the therapist who overestimates himself agree in their evaluations, yet these are not reality.

3. Integration: The action of the other person is adopted into one's own action scheme. This is in today's view the function of mirror neurons. "In his brain they activate his own motor functions, exactly the same as if he had executed the observed action himself" according to Bauer (2006, p. 26). This ability to observe the other person so that we can absorb his action into our action scheme, retrace it and, based on repeated experience, predict it, forms the basis for creating relationships.

4. Mutual relationship building: A creative act leads from a tele process to a tele relationship. When we evade each other in traffic in order to avoid a collision, it is based on relationship building by "tele". If we both swerve to the same side, the relationship has failed. For people to play together, the instant awareness of the other person, as tele is also called by Moreno, is the foundation of relationship creation.

When we face an opponent, tele is also important since we have to anticipate our opponent's next move, based on our observations, in order to react at the right moment and be successful. While we are hardly aware of this ability, it is soon noticeable when it is impaired, as will be obvious in the examples from therapy sessions.

Tele, transference and empathy

The delineation of tele versus transference and empathy is clear in psychodrama and consists in tele meaning the complete "Zweifühlung" or mutual awareness. Two people are simultaneously and adequately aware of each other. Transference and countertransference on the other hand are not based on instant awareness, but on one-sided imagining and expectation. Empathy is also one-sided.

Tele clearly distinguishes itself from transference and empathy by its reciprocal nature (Ameln, Gestmann & Kramer 2009). Leutz (1986) designates the perception of reality as tele. She states that this is not a given with transference and stresses that tele is always adequate, be it in a loving encounter or in a fight. In a fight it is just as important to sense the intentions of the opponent ("reality-adequate opposition") as in a mutual loving relationship.

appropriate

Tele (the reality-adequate perception) provides unconscious knowledge and is thereby part of intuition.

When tele is at work during the choosing of a role, one may get the impression that tele is transference or empathy. This stems from the fact that role choosing involves additional factors, such as degree of familiarity, transference, empathy and social justice. Often social fairness is a more important factor in choosing than tele, and role players are chosen because they have not played before, independent of the tele relationship.

Of course, work in psychodrama also involves transference, countertransference and projection as in music therapy and other psychotherapeutic methods, and special interventions such as scene changes can bring awareness of projections (see Chapter 9, Scene Change in Music Therapy).

Tele and role exchange

Tele is the primordial human mode for interactions and the basis for role exchange. Without tele no role exchange is successful. With the technique of role exchange, lost tele and lost resonance ability can be regenerated. Gradually, the simultaneous "I and you" experience can be experienced again in a reality-adequate manner, be it in a loving relationship with attraction or in a reality-correct experience of incompatibility. In music therapy the terms for these phenomena are synchronization and resonance. There is, however, some overlap between the terms tele, resonance, and synchronization.

2.3 Roles and Role Categories

To Moreno it was clear that humans start already in the embryonic stage to enter into a relationship with their environment as acting, behaving individuals and do this in at least one role. He believes that man takes on roles in the system he lives in and that spontaneous shaping of these roles already takes place prenatally (Leutz 1986). Moreno was convinced that an infant is born with role patterns. Karin Schumacher (1994) also describes infants as actors and communicators. Today the intrauterine relationship development by a fetus may be observed by ultrasound. Piontelli (1996) researched the intrauterine relationship development by twins and found that they continued their interaction after birth. This interaction had been influenced by their position in the uterus.

Roles

Roles are created very early and develop further through human interactions. These experiences are crucial for the personal interpretation of roles. Individuals move in a spectrum of total adaptation and uninhibited creation (Springer 1995). This view is similar to its expression in music therapy: "Between freedom and dependence lies a range of social adjustment and responsibility" (Hegi-Portmann, Lutz Hochreutener & Rüdisüli-Voerkel 2006, p. 41). Psychodrama deals with this social adjustment in the individual roles. In therapy this differentiated view helps to make good use of resources in well-cast roles, as well as to take on fixed or rejected roles in order to release blocked energy.

Role clusters

The diverse roles which we adopt at birth, and in part even before birth, form clusters, meaning that several roles melt into one. The role "baby" is already a cluster in which many roles are joined together: father's child, mother's child, grandchild, sibling, drinker, screamer, sleeper etc. Our roles are always clusters, at the workplace, in the family or in society. The breaking up of a cluster can bring crucial new insights and lead to growth. Music therapy is well suited for work with clusters. Music allows synchrony. The work with role clusters in music therapy is described in detail in Chapter 10.

Moreno's role categories and their counterparts in other concepts (Daniel Stern and Fritz Hegi)

In music therapy practice, the theory of role categories has proven to be very helpful. In particular, the choice of appropriate interventions is made easier. A patient's suffering can manifest itself in all spheres, and an understanding of the different spheres can facilitate access and change.

Moreno developed four role categories (also role levels). The basis for these was his careful observation of people. His concern was to consciously sense the different levels of human problems since symptoms can appear on all four levels and can point to effective interventions. He designated the physical/somatic as the first level from which the psychological level with self-awareness develops. With the recognition of a "You", the social level is set and, with language, the level of interpretation in which symbolism becomes possible is defined; he calls this the transcendent level. When therapy reaches the correct level it can provide direct access to suffering as well as resources.

Role categories represent different "emergence levels" (Krüger 1997, p. 57). Emergence means the surfacing of a new level of existence from a lower level, with a new quality. Krüger researched psychodramatic interventions with respect to these emergence levels and showed their correlation with illnesses.

In recent infant research one finds confirmation of Moreno's observations. Daniel Stern (2006) describes the development of infants with the "emergence of existence levels in the development of self-awareness." He also distinguishes four levels which are similar to Moreno's levels: first, the physical/somatic self that we are often unaware of. Next, circumstances, feelings, and intentions are remembered, and in the third phase the child is aware of him/herself and others. Finally, the ability to see the self objectively and to give it significance in the world so it may be shared with others, the phase of the verbal self, is entered.

Moreno, Krüger, and Stern agree: each of the four levels develops from the previous one and all remain active, none deteriorates with development.

Here an overview of the two models:

Moreno Role Categories	Stern Domains of Relatedness
4. Transcendent Roles	Verbal self
3. Social Roles	Subjective self
2. Psychological Roles	Core self
1. Somatic Roles	Emergent self

Table 1. Moreno's role categories and their corresponding concepts in Stern's Domains of Relatedness.

The distinction of levels in the warm-up phase and recognition of the level of the "problem role" can be useful in therapeutic processes, as discussed in Chapter 6, entitled "Warming up in Music Therapy Based on Psychodramatic Role Theory".

Finding that work with certain role categories can provide selective access to suffering and thereby intensify and improve the quality of therapy, motivated me to find analogous models for music therapy. During practical work some similarities between Moreno's role categories and the model of musical components according to Fritz Hegi (1998) became evident.

Moreno Role Categories	Hegi Components
Transcendent Roles	Form
Social Roles	Melody
Psychological Roles	Sound
Somatic Roles	Rhythm

Table 2. Moreno's Role Categories and Hegi's Components.

The parallels between the research results of Fritz Hegi and Daniel Stern may be viewed as follows:

– Rhythm is connected with biorhythms and life rhythms (Hegi 1998). Rhythm is therefore connected to somatic roles and the physical/somatic self.
– Sound intangibly fills space and connects with the realm of the senses (Hegi 1998). Sound is linked to psychological roles and the core self.
– Melody connects to memories and stories (Hegi 1998). It is connected to social roles or the subjective self.
– Form, the component of change and new creation (Hegi 1998), is connected to giving meaning, creating symbols, with transcendent roles and the verbal self.
– Dynamics are in my experience a polar indicator of energy and tension in all four role levels and are diagnostically revealing. Fritz Hegi classifies dynamics as relationship dynamics.

Hegi's view is helpful in therapeutic work. By focusing our attention on the individual components of music, we can use this knowledge in the diagnosis and selection of future therapeutic steps.

The bridge to other models of personality description (Stern, Hegi) should help clarify the concepts of Moreno's role theory on a different level. Details on how to stimulate a role category with music therapy and psychodrama interventions will be described in detail in Chapter 6.

2.4 Important Concepts in Psychodrama Work

In psychodrama one talks about materials and instruments and techniques. The instruments include, for example, the stage, the psychodrama group, the "double", the therapist, the "protagonist", the set, and the "social atom" or the "vignette". The materials also include all the sites, persons, and groups of people or forms of representation. Examples of techniques are "warming up", role reversal, sharing, feedback, role change, "doubling", "mirroring", in other words, the activities.

In practice the materials, instruments and techniques build a confluent entity. To examine their effect and use, the distinction between materials and techniques is not relevant; therefore I shall use the term psychodrama elements for both. This way confusion between psychodrama instruments and musical instruments is avoided.

Important psychodrama elements:

- **The stage:** In psychodrama the space is divided into spectator space/audience and stage. Real experienced situations as well as imagined ones are brought to the stage. With distance and new competence they can be re-lived and/or altered. The stage is an artificial as well as artistic situation. Here one can experiment/rehearse and vary things. Everything is possible, such as killing and loving. There are two stage rules: everything is "pretend", and hurting others is not allowed.

- **Warming up** in psychodrama is an energetic process to stimulate topics. It is performed at the beginning of a therapeutic session or is used during a session to mobilize energy. Warming up can also be used in study groups. Several types of interventions are available for example, conversation, sociometry, pictures or musical forms as described in Chapter 6. They are used according to the type of process chosen.

- **The protagonist:** A person who brings his/her topic to the stage is called the "protagonist". The protagonist is the creator, similar to a composer of music. The therapist accompanies and gives advice in adaption to the stage. By including the group members, repressed conflicts may be presented and, by using different elements, can be worked on together.

- **Scene** building is the phase in which the therapist arranges the stage with the protagonist and decides together with him/her which roles and props are needed. This is a crucial phase where the therapist is responsible for the direction. Here she has to be like a good director and advise the author/protagonist, anticipating the process of the play to follow. This is where the therapist can address repressed and dissociated matters and ask the protagonist acceptingly how he intends to present these parts. Even if the protagonist is defensive, questions from the therapist can lead to awareness of previously unrecognized parts of the self. Scene building supports the expression of self components. The psychological self-image of the protagonist is set up spacially and symbolically with help from the group members and/or objects.

Systemic therapy works on the basis of psychodramatic scene building, be it with vignettes or family presentation.

- **"Play/enactment"** is the action phase on the stage. The patient and therapist have the right to halt the play at any time, either to freeze it to hold the action for a moment in order to focus on an important image, or to view the scene from the audience. The play may also be ended in order to discuss it or to protect from re-traumatizing.

- **Change of scene** allows for a new interpretation of the topic. The time period can be changed, for example, from the present to a situation in childhood or from the present to a vision of the future. The change of scene also offers the possibility of showing different variations of a problem or exploring different solutions.

- **"Doubling"** in psychodrama essentially means that another person empathizes with the protagonist, e. g., the therapist who expresses what the patient may be thinking or feeling. The protagonist may also choose a double to represent him and allow him to view himself from a distance (from the auditorium) or with someone else playing his role (role exchange). **The double can also stand behind or next to the protagonist as an auxiliary ego to reinforce him or to bring out repressed parts.** If a protagonist acts very restrained in enacting a conflict, for example, the double may express repressed anger, rage or sadness. The protagonist is encouraged by the therapist to check the actions of the double for accuracy. As a rule the protagonist immediately rejects an inaccurate enactment.

- **Role exchange** is the taking on of a different role. In psychodrama one distinguishes between changing from one role to another (passively waiting, observer, attacker, calculating person) and role reversal between two relationship partners (e. g., teacher/student – student/teacher). Role exchange and role reversal have entirely different functions and effects. Role exchange, the ability to take on different roles and playing them well nuanced, is an important human ability in development, for example, for a woman to be a professional, mother, wife, neighbor, friend, and hostess. By changing roles, role flexibility is practiced and the development of identity promoted. Modifying roles that no longer work or which are fixed, allows for healthy changes and identity development.

- **Role reversal** takes place between partners. Role A is related to role B. It is of advantage to consider both roles during scene planning. The protagonist alternates between the two roles. With role reversal, empathy can be enhanced. Role reversal can also be used to clarify relationships and conflicts.

- **Sharing:** The group members and the therapist express how the play affects them personally. In contrast to psychoanalysis, which demands abstinence from the therapist, in psychodrama the therapist is asked to share if s/he feels personally affected. Since patients notice the effect on the therapist anyway by tele, but do not understand the reason, sharing by the therapist clarifies the underlying reasons for their observations or perceptions. The subject of the sharing consists of memories and feelings which were evoked by the play. Similarities and differences in personal experiences are recognized. The participants' observations are also validated and the participants can now "file" the personal consternation of the therapist and of the other group members. Sharing is always a personal experience as is remembering one's own biography and is therefore different from feedback. The sharing round pulls in all the participants, actors and spectators (see Ch. 5.4).

- **Feedback** means reporting a response to the play. Sharing and feedback originated in psychodrama and today are often used in pedagogic and therapeutic contexts. In psychodrama all group members participate in feedback. We can distinguish between the role feedback of the players and the identification feedback of the spectators and the director.

  With sharing having preceded feedback, the personal consternation of the participants has become transparent. The preceding sharing round emotionally unburdens the participants of their own memories and feeling and thereby directs the feedback more towards the protagonist. The perceptions of the role players are very revealing and this is used for setting up the family constellation. Feedback from the spectators often brings new points of view and insights.

- **Processing** is an analysis which is made with the group or patient in order to recognize the steps, repeat them, and reinforce them and to uncover connections.

- **Improvisational/spontaneous play** can be performed by some or all group members. Nothing is planned. The director can demand role exchanges. If needed he can take on a role and lead from that role. If one works with a co-therapist, one person takes the lead counseling role and the other takes the weakest position, weaker than the weakest member of the group, to be able to offer strategies or solutions and to facilitate transformations. If the development of the weakest member of a group is not supported, the danger arises that this member could leave the group or regress.

- **Conserves** in psychodrama are "preserved" written or other lasting creative works. Grete Leutz (1986) believes that these works, conserved creations, mark a culture and are therefore needed. A universe consisting merely of spontaneity and creativity would be a universe without a world. With this she points out that we live with and from our cultural heritage, the "conserves". If everything were only spontaneous and creative, it would be incomprehensible like the universe.

  Among the cultural conserves applied in psychodrama are fairy tales, poems of all types, pictures, compositions, traditional songs and sayings, but also oral traditions and role behavior. Conserves are preserved end products of a preceding creative process. They may also stimulate more people to become creative.

- **Sociometry:** J. L. Moreno developed the beginnings of sociometry while working as a camp physician during World War I. He recorded the social conditions of the camp inhabitants and compared the results with their case histories. He noticed that individuals who were long-term patients lived in difficult conditions with anger, tension and quarrels. The happier and healthier ones shared cabins with relatives, acquaintances or new friends. He was able to prove a connection between health and environment. Unfortunately he was not allowed to move refugees around based on his sociometric findings. Yet he continued to work on sociometric and group dynamics research, on human attraction and rejection, and developed several sociometric tests (Leutz 1986).

Group therapy without sociometry is now unthinkable. It is also applied in pedagogy. In therapy attention and therapeutic engagement is focused on the losers of sociometry, the rejected, the isolated, unwanted and neglected individuals of the group. Their health is in danger.

There are different sociometric elements, for instance, "selections/choices". They can display the energy of a group, the position of a person in the group and various enmeshments. Other elements such as the social atom are mainly used for diagnosis.

- **The social atom** is an important diagnostic tool in psychodrama. Moreno took the Greek word atomos (=not divisible) to designate the relationship structure which surrounds the core of the individual from birth on. Every person is enveloped in such a social atom (Leutz 1986) where the atom is an inseparable part of the personality.

  If from birth on we have a father, mother, grandparents, perhaps siblings, these have a representation within us which corresponds to a role, e. g., mother's child, father's child, and grandchild. Usually the patient is asked to see himself as the center, as the core and to draw the people next to him that spontaneously come to mind, using for example, circles for women and squares for men, with their distance corresponding to his feelings for them. The social atom is constantly changing. New individuals are added. There are losses, especially in old age or after emigration. The social atom is always a snapshot. Individual people in the social atom light up and become extinguished, come closer and get more distant like stars in a night sky. Dead individuals can suddenly become important, distant ones can shine brightly. Further details may be found in Chapter 13 "The Social Atom in Music Therapy".

- **The cultural atom** is a further evolution of the social atom and contains cultural roles, for example, profession, neighbor, citizen, not only as social roles but beyond this as transcendent roles. "Profession" is not limited to a work situation, but rather represents a calling. A neighbor in the cultural atom is not a certain relationship with a person next door, it is "neighborliness". In life crises and phases of searching for meaning, the cultural atom can uncover causes and encourage new steps (see "The Cultural Atom in Music Therapy" Ch. 14).

2.5 The Depth Psychology Background of Psychodrama

Recognition of connections between psychodrama elements, problems and functions facilitates the choice of interventions during the leading of a session, as well
as understanding in hindsight during the processing of protocols.

The depth psychology effect of psychodrama elements which Moreno developed by observing the behavior patterns of his fellow men and which he named in
his theory, is still a subject of research. Reinhard Krüger (1997) deals mainly with
the depth psychology effects of each element and describes the many-sided depth
psychology functions.

For example Michael Schacht (2004) describes the structure formation through
role exchange, role reversal and sharing. This allows the generation of emotional
resonance, gaining of perspective, and the ability to experience closeness to other
people.

Michael Wieser (2004) describes some evidence of effects of psychodrama from
different studies in different disorders. As factors in addition to the effects of psychodrama, he mentions the effects of the therapeutic relationship, the personality
of the therapist, and environmental factors as well as the private and social network
of the patient. These factors, together with psychodrama, can result in positive and
negative combinations, which complicate the research. This is also true for music
therapy and for all psychodynamic therapies, and makes interpretation of effects
more difficult.

3 Parallels between Music Therapy and Psychodrama

The common scientific background of these two methods is instrumental to their integration. Current teaching opinions for music therapy and psychodrama draw mainly on the same scientific base and have many similarities. Table 5 shows how striking the parallels are between the two media, music and drama, regarding their therapeutic elements. The term tele in psychodrama overlaps with the concept of "resonance" in music therapy. Equally important are spontaneity and creativity, both being central to the two methods.

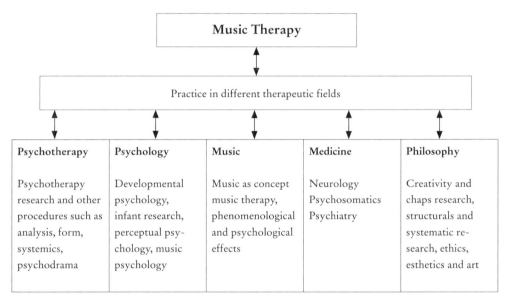

Psychotherapy	Psychology	Music	Medicine	Philosophy
Psychotherapy research and other procedures such as analysis, form, systemics, psychodrama	Developmental psychology, infant research, perceptual psychology, music psychology	Music as concept music therapy, phenomenological and psychological effects	Neurology Psychosomatics Psychiatry	Creativity and chaps research, structurals and systematic research, ethics, esthetics and art

Table 3. Music Therapy and Scientific Background

At the center of the scientific background of psychodrama are the social sciences. In addition to therapy, psychodrama is also applied in education, counseling and supervision. Therefore the psychology of learning and the more important social sciences are examined here. Music research, per se, is not a topic of this book.

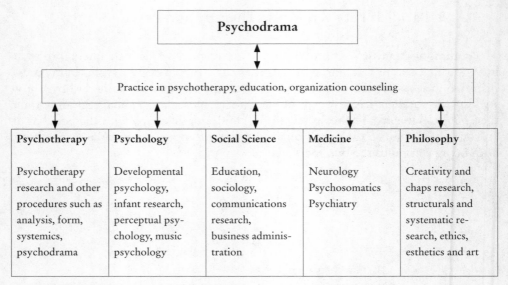

Table 4. Psychodrama and its Scientific Background

The main common areas are neurological research, developmental psychology, creativity research, and systems and structure research. Because improvisation, which is the spontaneous, creative, and playful answer to the unexpected, is so central to both methods, psychodrama elements can easily be integrated into music therapy.

3.1 Psychodrama Elements and their Parallels in Music Therapy

In psychodrama many elements of drama (staged stories) have been pointedly extracted, applied as therapeutic methods and studied. In music therapy one finds equivalent techniques.

Psychodrama	Music Therapy
Warm-up	Tuning, warm-up play
Stage	Stage
Scene setting	Instrument selection
Props	Instruments
Scene acting	Musical play
Change of scene	New musical movement
Role reversal	Instrument exchange
Role exchange	Instrument change

Table 5. Psychodrama Elements and their Equivalents in Music Therapy

Additional elements which were developed and studied in psychodrama can easily be adapted for music therapeutic interventions. In music therapy, for example, during sharing the consternation or dismay of the participants can be expressed with musical instruments. Feedback may be in the form of applause, resonance or echo; doubling can be arranged with joining in unison, by a choir, or with an instrument register like that in an orchestra; replays, or playing an orchestra conductor can result in mirroring.

3.2 Moreno's Tele in Psychodrama and the Concept of Resonance in Music Therapy

The term tele in psychodrama has been discussed in the preceding chapter. In music therapy tele corresponds mainly to the aspect of resonance. Moreno understood tele as the current of feelings that flows between two or several people. He worked with it in group therapy by letting the protagonist freely choose his players by "sensing" who would be suited for a certain role. With well-developed tele this practice leads to adequate selections. Often participants sense in advance which role they will be asked to play.

Bauer (2006, p. 106) describes this phenomenon as follows (*translated from German*): "Mirror neurons provide a common social resonance space, because the feelings and actions of an individual activate a mirroring system of neurons in the observers, as if the latter were feeling or acting the same, even though they are actually only observers."

To understand resonance in music therapy, the phenomenon of tele (in German: *Zwei- und Mehrfühlung*) has been described, among other things, as, "To be on the same wave length", meaning a fundamental (underlying everything), primary, non-material, heartfelt connection. "Resonance is the basic pulsation of attachment/closeness, an energetic emotion which grabs us" (Gindl 2002, p. 68).

Resonance and tele are overlapping terms. Barbara Gindl (2002) calls resonance a sensory event which allows us to tune into another person and oscillate with him or her. She writes that the phenomenon of resonance is a fundamental principle of life and of living systems in general, and central to the success of therapy. If we compare this statement about resonance with Moreno's tele concept, we can see the close relationship between music therapy and psychodrama. Since tele is as crucial to the success of psychodrama as resonance is to success with music therapy, interventions with both methods aim in the same direction, and therefore lend themselves well to being integrated.

Tele in psychodrama and resonance in music therapy are phenomena which bridge the distance between two or more people and are in part responsible for group cohesion.

3.3 Tele and Synchronization

Anticipation, called tele in psychodrama, is a precondition for being able to synchronize with other beings and to establish a relationship. Karin Schumacher (1994) found that the beginning of human transient oscillation begins before birth. Moreno was already convinced in the 1940s that, likewise, tele begins around birth and that it can be seen as the basis for all healthy human interactions. He saw infants as creative communicators, not just as beings thrown into the world. He holds that this is apparent from the first breastfeeding. From the sensation of hunger the infant steps into the role of eater without a preceding identification/imitation step.

If the capacity for resonance is absent in one of the interacting persons, then tele is disrupted (Leutz 1986). Karin Schumacher (1994) confirmed these findings and added that every person, even the autistic child, communicates.

Moreno describes tele as the ability to anticipate, outside of emotions. He thereby describes a form of resonance which we also find mentioned by Bauer (2006) as "activity of the mirror neurons outside of emotional resonance, as the capacity to anticipate and to perform an action in the imagination." This function is of vital importance, not only in street traffic.

Beyond musical and technical training, tele, as the ability to synchronize and anticipate, is a quality required by musicians in order to play together and to simultaneously develop their playing together. Well developed mirror neurons, the ability to sense what comes next, to be moved internally, mutual empathy, are conditions for every good musical ensemble. This also occurs when musicians do not know each other, are not in a personal relationship, and no conductor is present.

Bauer (2006, p. 12) describes this sensing of others as the output of mirror neurons. "The result is that between people who interact, a continuous, largely synchronous, common attention is established – a phenomenon which is called 'joint attention' in neurobiology." Regarding the significance of this function in daily life he writes,

"The function of mirror neurons is to help people feel comfortable and secure, move confidently in traffic, to learn, and to incorporate events affecting others into one's own. When this capacity is absent, serious problems can arise" (translated from German, Bauer 2006, p. 13).

Although current understanding of the function of mirror neurons may not be as clear as Bauer presents it, humans and animals do possess this capacity for sensing the feelings and intentions of others. The movements of a flock of birds in the air and of a school of fish in the water, where even at high speed there is never a collision, are wonderful images of this neuronal ability which still holds many secrets.

Karin Schumacher (1994; 2007) describes problems of synchronization in therapies with autistic children and shows methods of intervention that stimulate synchronization. Through music as a medium, music therapy offers possibilities for developing the capacity for synchronization in many areas.

Building on the background of modern neurology research, psychotherapeutic interventions complement music therapy based around the tele phenomenon.

Moreno was convinced that tele deserved major attention in therapy. Music therapy in turn is concerned with resonance phenomena and with developing new approaches. These may be supplemented by psychodrama elements; for example, through role reversal, emotional resonance can be relearned. In neuro-rehabilitation one finds patients with frontal lobe problems which cause them to have extremely stressful insecurities. When the unconscious tele process and synchronization no longer function spontaneously after a brain injury, the use of music therapy supplemented with psychodrama elements can allow the therapist to observe how small partial functions may be rebuilt, resulting in the patient gaining more confidence (see "Example from Practice in Neuro-Rehabilitation" at the end of Chapter 3.6).

3.4 Tele, Resonance and Diagnostics

In diagnostics, tele is only of limited use because empathy is difficult to measure. However, one can analyze aspects where tele plays a role. This includes areas such as personal interactions, the capacity for role reversal, the socio-emotional relationship system, the social network, and problems with spontaneity and creativity. One should be aware that tele is never an isolated component, but that other factors, such as group dynamics and transference and countertransference, play a part as well.

The following quote describes how imprecisely tele is used in diagnostics:

"If with diagnostics […] we denote not only the classification, but generally the process which provides a counselor or therapist with information about the state of health of a client, as well as the reasons for his actions, then this too – what psychodramatists designate as tele – is a diagnostic tool. It is questionable how consciously this process of diagnostics and intervention planning takes place" (Ameln, Gerstmann & Kramer 2009, p. 152).

If we view tele as an aspect of the phenomenon of resonance, music therapy diagnostics is more relevant. Resonance and the capacity for resonance are consciously applied in music therapy as diagnostic tools and have been well researched. Different music therapists have discussed diagnostics based on resonance problems, and have developed interventions aimed at improving resonance ability. These include, for example Isabelle Frohne-Hagemann (1993) in "Musiktherapeutische Diagnostik und Manual nach ICD 10" (Music Therapeutic Diagnostics and Manual following ICD 10) and Karin Schumacher (1994) with "EBQ, Einschätzung der Beziehungsqualität" (Evaluation of Relationship Quality). Additionally, Barbara Gindl (2002) describes problems caused by poorly developed resonance ability. She describes these as the suffering from the lack of responsiveness and from one's own lack of resonance, non-feeling, non-sensing, emptiness. Such individuals, she writes, often cannot feel the emotional 'being touched', nor do they allow themselves to feel it and thus cannot initiate and regulate it.

With their goal of promoting resonance, psychodramatic interventions are perfectly suited for music therapy, including their additional aspects, for example, conscious role exchange and resonance phenomena in groups during sociometric role selections.

3.5 Tele, Resonance and Spirituality

For Moreno it was clear that tele also has a spiritual side. He mentions repeatedly that tele is also a fundamental, loving acceptance of other people, and that by caring, one offers others a deep benevolence and wishes others pure prosperity. This view also holds for Gindl regarding eagerness for resonance in music therapy.

B. Gindl (2002, p. 157) states "– *the attitude of love, dedication, and encounter corresponds to my understanding of a therapeutically healing attitude*", and she asks herself if such an attitude may be experienced without the therapist finding himself held accountable for something greater, more complete.

"*It is the creative world process that we are all part of*" (Leutz 1986, p. 57). J. L. Moreno had the opinion that the "He-God" had become a "*You-God*" through Jesus Christ who thus becomes accessible through feelings. He takes this further by viewing the future of the planet as depending on the conscious integration of man into the world process, and integration of the creative world process into the conscious actions of man. Leutz notes that man is seen as a part of a whole in the cosmos, not small and powerless, but creatively involved and responsible. In her view the therapist is not only open to tele, but is a conscious and creative part of the relationship. This view of man is a good fit for music therapy where we encounter patients creatively in improvisations. It also fits today's view of the world in which humans are the cause of climate change and destruction of the environment. Creativity and responsible actions are in demand.

Example from practice in Neuro-Rehabilitation: rebuilding tele, meaning of life, and synchronization

Patient T. is 27 years old; he has a severe frontal lobe brain lesion as a result of being hit by a car. He is maladjusted and suicidal. Currently, he is in a second 3-month stay at the rehabilitation clinic and attends music therapy twice a week.

Developing synchronization

1st Session: Despite the fact that Mr. T. moves very well, has no paralysis, and shows no signs of the accident, he feels bad and cannot imagine walking on a street again where people move around freely, and where there are cars. He says that he has become a 'nobody'. His life in the clinic makes no sense to him. He drums randomly with his fingers and sits at the large drum which appeals to him. Initially I accompany Mr. T. in his improvisations, playing in synchrony. Even at a very slow tempo, he is not capable of imitating simple movements synchronously. I adapt my playing to accompany his beat.

2nd and 3rd Sessions: Mr. T. starts every session with the complaint that he is a 'nobody' and then starts playing on the table drum. My regular and emotionally matched interplay leads the patient to a point where he spontaneously and unconsciously begins to adjust his playing. When I change something, he begins to guess, based on motions, what comes next and can reproduce it. For example, we can change the timing (meter) or play a loud final drum beat together. This pleases him and fills him with new hope. The big step in the third session is for Mr. T. to observe the therapist, and together with her, play the same drum movements with similar intensity, at a very slow tempo.

Access to resources through roles

4th Session: Again Mr. T. starts the session with, "I'm a nobody." This time I answer, "To me you are patient T., not Mr. 'Nobody'. To be a patient is your job, your role now, and you can play it in different ways. Perhaps you have other parts to play?" I list a few. He says, "Yes, I am also a boyfriend, but that is difficult, and I am also a roommate in a 4-person room, and that is also difficult!"

He wants to act the role of the patient and chooses the large drum as symbol for the patient. He beats it slowly, strongly and regularly. Then he looks at me. I start to play with him. At the end he says, "That felt good!" For feedback I say: "I heard a patient who has the right to take his time, and to be accompanied and taken care of."

Transfer through roles

5th Session: In the next session, Mr. T. expands his patient role creatively. No word about being a 'nobody'. He allows me, according to his own wishes, to accompany him musically. He relaxes. My feedback: "You have wishes and know what you want, this pleases me. "After this session he succeeds in transferring his patient role to the clinic. He can more easily accept being accompanied by a nurse and feels less degraded and powerless; he feels that he can shape the relationships. The clinic staff notes in their report that patient T. has become much more cooperative.

Recapturing the meaning of life by differentiating roles

Sessions 6–9: Mr. T. differentiates his patient role further as "walking patient" and "learning patient". In music therapy he learns to be more self-aware and to better adjust demands on himself to his abilities – not a small undertaking when the planning and decision making organ, the frontal lobe, is impaired.

Dealing with love and sexuality

10th Session: After a visit from his girlfriend, he wants to play his role as a boyfriend. He is afraid of his own sexual arousal and loss of control. Playing the metallophone he rediscovers through music his tenderness which he had suppressed out of fear. With the musical dialogue he practices facing his limitations and fear. The weekly meetings with his girlfriend are becoming more relaxed. He can talk to her about his fear and his problems.

Reducing aggression and improving impulse control through role reversal

15th Session: Mr. T. acts out his problematic role as roommate very aggressively on a djembe (African drum). He stops soon and says: "I can't stand these people anymore!" Daily proximity to men whom he judges unpredictable makes him angry. In music therapy he succeeds in exchanging the role of roommate P with his own and thereby empathising with roommate P. Through this role reversal, he recognizes his irritability and aggression, and can admit to it. With help from the caretaker he can distance himself when he becomes agitated.

From the next report I learn that he does not quarrel with his roommates any more, that he distances himself, and that he does not compare himself with others as often.

Synchronization and social competence

Sessions 16–18: His progress in empathy and in motor skill synchronization soars. He now can improvise together with me without effort. At the same time he is getting better at performing role reversals, in music therapy as well as at the clinic. He begins to sympathize with his roommates. In these last sessions he learns to improvise together in a relaxed manner.

Therapy conclusion

Sessions 19 and 20: Mr. T. would like to play all the roles once more. At the end of the therapy he says that playing the patient roles on the drum gave him great pleasure and helped him to accept his situation.

Process

At first, the ability to synchronize (1st and 3rd sessions), then the resources and insight into his illness (4th session) are worked on. The jump in progress after the 5th session is striking. Perhaps social transfer and the growing ability to synchronize promote each other.

The patient's neurological recovery is partially successful. Aggression which initially caused daily friction has become a driving force for the music therapeutic activities. Patient T. says that as long as he does not have a handle on it, he wants to come to therapy (understanding of his illness and the role of "learning patient").

Occurrence of resonance in music therapy, unison improvisations, mutual simultaneous synchronisation during drumming, and emotional resonance all improve as soon as patient T. plays an instrument in a deliberately chosen role.

Transfer to daily life is supported by musical role playing. Patient T. takes the experimental acting from therapy, tied to a role, consciously into his daily situations. As the "learning patient" he can concentrate on himself and his self-awareness when something happens too fast or becomes too much or too heavy, in contrast to the role of "Mr. Nobody" in which he is resentful, depressed, and acts aggressively. On the metallophone he finds his tenderness again and takes it into daily life in the role of friend and lover. Transfer to the love relationship becomes possible.

Mr. T. has become more flexible. He has developed his role as patient, boyfriend, and as roommate. His rebuilt self-image encourages him to practice, and supports the regaining of synchronization. This therapeutic work moves in areas of functional and psychodynamic music therapy, supported by psychodramatic elements. The suicidal Mr. Nobody has evolved into a self determined young man who, despite impairments from an accident, is willing to face life.

When a patient with a brain injury can express his different roles in musical improvisations, discern them and creatively modify them, transfer of learned functions to daily life is facilitated. The roles are like containers in which one can carry experiences from the therapy room to everyday life.

In many cases the success achieved with patient T. is not possible. Often, when brain functions are not re-established, severe impairment remains, invisible from outside, but manifested by emotional, social, and motor insecurity, and often poor impulse control. These individuals cannot anticipate events. Bauer (2006, p. 13) expresses this situation as follows: "Without the intuitive certainty over the immediate consequences of a given situation, living together by humans is quite unimaginable" (translated from German). A difficult invisible condition!

3.6 Spontaneity, Creativity and Conserves

As a rule, impairments in spontaneity are rooted in fear. This limits readiness for action and blocks access to creative solutions and their application to life situations, which in turn leads to limitations in life quality and to various psychological and somatic problems. In music therapy and psychodrama one "plays or acts". In the protected space of play, creativity and spontaneity can unfold.

Spontaneity

Spontaneity, the immediate readiness to get involved with unknown, new, unusual, and tempting things, appears to be the result of several factors acting together. Without spontaneity musical improvisation is unthinkable. Frohne-Hagemann (2001) describes improvisation in music therapy as a spontaneous medium in which the patient finds himself completely in the present, without time to control his impulses. This allows unconscious impulses, dissociated parts and repressed material to become audible in improvisation, before the inner censor has time to suppress them. The patient thus reveals valuable aspects of his problems.

Psychodrama works on the same basis. The flow of actions in the play does not allow time to control impulses. Lack of available spontaneity manifests itself in fixation on roles, avoidance of conserved roles (traditional, learned behaviour patterns) or automatisms. Conspicuousness and abnormalities of life competencies become noticeable.

Psychodramatic acting relieves fear because of its "pretend" play and can therefore raise the level of spontaneity, as long as there is a trusting relationship with the therapist. Musical improvisation can also provide the function of a "no danger zone" to relieve fear.

With "warming up", an energetic process to stimulate topics, the willingness to act and thereby exhibit spontaneity can also be enhanced.

Creativity

Creativity, man's power to produce, is central to both methods. It is the force which balances chaos, order, and chance (Hegi 1998). Musical improvisation is a good medium for developing creativity.

Donald Woods Winnicott (1985, 2005) writes that we observe that people either live creatively and find life worth living, or that they are not capable of living creatively and doubt life's value. He holds that unstructured experience and creative motor and sensory impulses, the raw materials for acting and playing, should be used. The whole human experience of play is built on this basis. However, the play has to be reflected on, for only then can it become a part of the structured individual personality (Winnicott 1985, p. 76–77). Music therapy and psychodrama are also built on this foundation.

Nordoff and Robbins (1977, 2007) called their method "Creative Music Therapy". They observed the qualities of their creative music therapeutic interventions which helped the development of children from different backgrounds (Pfahl, Koch-Temming 2005, p. 43–45), Sandra Lutz (2008, p. 164) sees, among other things, self-discovery and self-development as functions of creative playing in music therapy. She confirms the experience of "causality" which leads to taking on responsibility.

Klaus Lammers (2004, p. 222) formulates this aspect as follows: "It is always about helping the patients in their power to act, i. e., to support them in regaining the strength to act." To accomplish this, one has to guarantee creative blossoming, and the techniques have to be open to different possible outcomes.

Both music therapy and psychodrama work with creativity, the force which helps us shape our life between predictable and chance events, to cross solidified borders and to create new order. To create new order, old bounderies have to be destroyed. To undo fixations and to stimulate creativity, and with it joy and meaning in life, it is important to go back to the rudimentary origin of the play experience. This does not exclude contact with works of art in therapy. Creativity in art is a struggle. This struggle can stimulate creativity or it can impede it. "The struggle for wholeness and perfect form demands the yes to imperfection, otherwise it becomes self-destructive. Beauty, harmony, perfection – these are demands which can destroy spontaneity and creativity" (Fausch 1989, p. 29). The use of finished art products is secondary in music therapy and psychodrama. In psychodrama works of art are called "conserves".

Conserves

As far as the use of conserves is concerned, music therapy has come closer to psychodrama. In psychodrama existing texts, prescribed actions or composed music have often been used intentionally, but have never been seen as "receptive" psychodrama. Fritz Hegi (2010) now largely removes this distinction, writing that since music therapy is about the ability to experience music, the distinction between composed music and improvisation is secondary. Both conserves and improvisation have their justification in the right place. However, in music therapy as well as in psychodrama, creative play in the moment is far more important.

4 Overview of Effects and Functions of Psychodrama Elements in Music Therapy

For effective intervention by a therapist, knowledge of the possible functions of interventions is necessary since almost all psychodrama elements have multiple functions. Often, there are several elements available for a given function. The psychodrama literature describes these functions and effects in detail (Anzieu 1984; Fürst, Ottomeyer & Prucker 2004; Dieckmann 1998; Krüger 1997).

The list in Table 6 gives an overview of the elements, with notes about their functions, effects, and indications. The allocations are not meant to be recipes, but are hints and studied qualities which can assist with meaningful integration of psychodramatic elements. An example from practice of a child's therapy is analyzed by looking at the functions of the elements, showing how elements from music therapy are used and what results they can produce.

All elements may be used in group or individual therapy. The following example from practice shows the confluence of music therapy and psychotherapy. Starting with Chapter 5, the elements from the table will be presented separately. The examples from practice, and hints for methods, as well as suggestions for ways of playing/acting, should facilitate understanding and application in practice.

4.1 Overview of Effects and Functions of Elements

Elements	Functions, Effects, Indications
Stage/auditorium	<ul><li>Play space, everything is possible</li><li>Transition space for language and music</li><li>Regression and actual age</li><li>Imagination and reality</li><li>Transition area for transfer from therapy to everyday life</li><li>For the spectators: identification with the performers</li><li>With distance from the enactment, more awareness</li></ul>
Scene building and instrument selection	<ul><li>During setting up of stage, clarification of situations</li><li>Role assignment and role explanation/clarification</li><li>Bring dissociations to the stage (symbolically, by the therapist)</li><li>Identity experience: all this belongs to me!</li></ul>
Scene change equivalent in music therapy: new movement	<ul><li>Presentation of transferences in parallel situations</li><li>Presentation of similar situations in different stages of life</li><li>Parallels from present with situations in family of origin, shown from dreams and reality</li><li>Development of a path from actual to the desired state</li><li>Expose repressions by repetition in different scenes</li><li>Find meaning in life</li><li>Develop perspectives (yesterday, today, tomorrow, in 10 years)</li></ul>
Doubling	<ul><li>Discern relationship patterns</li><li>Express dissociations through therapist or a double, promoting awareness</li><li>Strengthen ego functions (auxiliary ego)</li><li>Fear reduction</li><li>Support of boundaries and ability to deal with conflict</li></ul>
Role change with the same instrument or change of instrument	<ul><li>Support of self worth</li><li>Present and recognize values (traditional, acquired)</li><li>Make repressions audible</li><li>Displacement awareness</li><li>Capture, expression, and assignment of free floating parts with an instrument</li><li>Try new things</li></ul>
Role reversal, instrument exchange Never in cases of abuse! Danger of identification with the aggressor and retraumatization	<ul><li>Expand experience of identity</li><li>Experience dissociations</li><li>Integrate dissociations by playing dissociated components</li><li>Empathy support</li><li>Strengthen You-recognition</li><li>Recognize internal roles and amplifications</li><li>Relationship work and relationship clarifications</li><li>Remodeling of fixed relationship patterns, expanding relationship knowledge</li></ul>

Elements	Functions, Effects, Indications
Sharing	• Promote self-awareness • Unburden group members of pent-up feelings by playing • Stimulate group members who are spectators • Encourage degree of familiarity and trust in the group • Create connections through problems; one is not alone in a difficult situation (Self help group dynamics) • Promote acceptance • Stimulate individual processes in groups through identification with roles on stage
Feedback	• Develop respect and attention; all want to be noticed • Support self-evaluation • Reduce energy, beneficial in cases of excessive agitation by participants • Convey and focus energy • Ease critical group situations, can provide security • Diagnostically: can point out identification with the aggressor • Integrate changes • Create connections • Facilitate transfer from therapy to daily life

Table 6. Psychodrama Elements with their Functions and Effects

4.2 Detailed Example of the Use of Psychodrama Elements in Music Therapy

The material below shows how psychodrama elements can be applied to music therapy to create the melding of music therapeutic and psychotherapeutic interventions. Only excerpts from session protocols which contain psychodramatic interventions were chosen. For a better overview, psychodrama elements are in bold text. Multiple music therapeutic interventions are described only where they occurred in connection with psychodrama elements. Music therapy sessions without psychodrama elements are not described in detail.

Example from practice using integration of psychodrama elements for a child Music Therapy in Youth Psychiatry.

Patient Claudio is 11 years old and has just arrived from a speech therapy school to an inpatient youth psychiatry facility due to life-threatening, violent outbursts (knife attacks on smaller children). At 4 years of age he suffered a severe concussion with possible brain injury from being hit by a car. It is not clear how much of Claudio's speech problems and behavior abnormalities are due to the brain injury. His parents are divorced, both are remarried; the father with a neighbor and the mother with a former friend. Therapy lasted a total of 2 years. Claudio is athletic, slim and rather short. He has a hoarse voice and closes his throat before exhaling. He attends music therapy and speech therapy once a week.

Session 1: The lump on the heart

Warming up: In the first session I ask him (as I usually do), "Why are you here at the clinic?" Claudio: "You know that – didn't you read my file?" After telling him that the reason is never in the files, he answers, "I am here because I have a 'lump' on my heart." "Where does it come from?" I ask. "Others threw it on it." "Who was it?" I ask. Claudio shrugs his shoulders and remains silent.

Play: I suggest playing "The lump on the heart".

Roles: The heart and the lump.

Setting up the scene: He is directed to choose an instrument for the first **role**, the heart. He chooses a beautiful, soft pillow with a cashmere case and puts it on the **stage**. The stage is a large, soft rug. For the second **role**, the lump, he picks out a conga which is in the room, wraps it in a cloth, and throws it roughly onto the pillow. Actions are fast! I **double**, "The lump almost crushes the heart". Claudio answers, "Yes, it almost crushes me, and at night I can't breathe and almost suffocate."

Claudio's voice gets even hoarser. He takes only short breaths. His chest stiffens between inhalation and exhalation, his throat tightens. In the **role reversal** with the heart he says, "It is so heavy!" In the **role reversal** with the lump, "The others threw me!"

Feedback: I tell Claudio, that the burden he suffers appears to be very large, and that he presents his situation and the reason for his clinic stay very well.

Process: Claudio has connected openly. He has easily accepted the **scene setting**. He has presented his central problem in somatic terms (heart, crushed, suffocating) with empathy and thereby shown insight to his problem. He chose a beautiful pillow as his heart. This speaks for self regard. He wrapped the conga into a cloth and thereby expressed lack of clarity about the lump. He did a **role reversal** with both parts and easily accepted the enactment.

Sessions 2 to 7: Warming up with the alphorn

At the beginning of the next session, I suggest playing the alphorn to allow him to gain energy on the **somatic level** through his breathing. Breathing can often stimulate access to repressed feelings, especially aggression and grief. Claudio does not react this way. After playing the alphorn he is calm and open. He likes playing the alphorn, and for the next sessions he wants to start with it every time. Following that, he usually wants to tell me what happened during the week, and what he has planned for the weekend. These are the subjects: vacation with his father, vacation with his mother, "my room" (boundary problems with the roommates), and nightmares.

Session 8: Contract killing nightmare

Warm-up: Claudio plays the alphorn and then tells me the nightmare he had previous night. "I am lying in bed as two young men sneak into my room. They are taller than I. Their job is to kill me. I wake up soaked in sweat and filled with fear."

Play: Murder contract

Roles: Claudio the dreamer, Claudio asleep in the dream, two young men with the contract to kill him.

Scene setting: In building the scenery it is important that Claudio represent Claudio dreaming (reality level), and the dream self which is to be killed, separately. The play is work on three levels, reality and the therapy session, the dreamer in his room, and the dream level. This is not easy for Claudio since he lies in bed as the dreamer, as well as the sleeper. So I let him choose two blankets. One of them represents his bed, from where he can see the other bed with Claudio dreaming and getting murdered in the dream.

Claudio wants to play the role psychodramatically and instead of using instruments as symbols, use pillows for his role and that of the two murderers. He plays all the **roles**. In the **role reversal** with the young men he says, "We have to do it! We don't know why, but it is an order!" As the dreamer, he lies stiff with fear. I go near him and try **doubling**, "You can't do this to me!" He does not react. My next attempt is, "Who sent you?" At this point Claudio gets up and leaves the stage. He wants to finish the play quickly and wants to talk.

We sit down on chairs in the **spectator/audience** area. He tells me about his Christmas. He visited his father who said, "I can't give you a present because I have to give your mother so much money!" (Alimony). The two stepsons (children of the father's second wife) had, of course, received presents from him. He said that he had to watch this, and that it was very sad. He is angry with his mother, "Why does she need so much money?" He says that Christmas was a very bad time for him. As therapist, I feel more the anger against the father and sadness about the impaired relationship with his mother, thwarted by the father.

Feedback: The hour is almost up and we have only very little time left. My feedback: "You look disappointed; are you annoyed at your mother? I am annoyed with your father for acting the way he did on Christmas. What he has to pay your mother is a matter of the courts. It has nothing to do with the Christmas presents!"

Process: Claudio reveals an incomprehensible threat in his dream – the contract to murder the "sleeping child". Then he tells the story about Christmas which touches me. (I find the father's behavior sadistic. He purposely makes the child suffer.) He creates a serious solidarity conflict for the son. The father accuses the mother, and immediately Claudio's feelings turn against her. The second part of the Christmas vacation, at his mother's, also becomes a negative experience, because he is angry with her. Here he is conflicted again. The sadness is over the beloved father whom he misses. The anger is with the mother who looks after him and protects him. With her, he is not afraid of loss of love, therefore anger is possible. Could the dissociated part of the father be commissioning the murder? The two boys whom he saw getting their presents were previously his friends, neighbors, and daily playmates before the parents' divorce. How can he love them now? Claudio's love needs to be killed. Did Claudio sense an intra-psychic murder? In the father's new relationship, at the new location, he is superfluous. The father wants to present an "intact family" in the village. Therefore, Claudio is only allowed to call him by his first name, and has to pretend to be a nephew, while the stepbrothers may call him father (decision by the father!). Here too, Claudio is divided – he is "only" sad and his anger is directed at his father's new wife. He says that it is all her fault. I understand that Claudio suffers an unbearable tension, and I describe it in the report.

Sessions 9 to 18: Setting the scene for the dissociation/split, and working with the environment

Almost every time before his session, Claudio plays the alphorn for 10 minutes – an intensive workout. Then he talks about the events of the past week. His chest is getting less tight and his voice clearer. He likes me and likes coming to therapy. I could be thinking, "A wonderful, successful therapy! I am a very good therapist!"

With his roommates he creates terror, is intolerant, chokes a younger boy dangerously, and wishes to kill an educator, wanting her to suffer as long as possible. He splits or dissociates between events with roommates and therapy. In our relationship he is only the good child. Important issues never enter the stage in therapy. This is evident in conversations with social workers. They report that he praises the therapist who understands him so well, in contrast to them, who are all 'dumb.' Their report about Claudio's behavior and my report need to be reconciled. We can't allow the split between "the good therapist" and the "mean educators" or the other way round, into "inadequate therapist" with the "candy job" who only makes the work of the educators more difficult, and "capable educators" who perform the "decisive work". We cannot support Claudio's tendency to divide. It will lessen his chance for recovery. His tendency to separate will get worse. I show the educators my esteem for their hard work, and for tolerating Claudio's murderous anger, and I point to the split in Claudio's mind. Here psychodrama offers me **scenery development** and **feedback**. With Reinhard Krüger, my supervisor, I have learned that as a therapist I am responsible for bringing good and bad objects to the stage. Whether or not the patient uses them for his play is up to him. It is not a matter of forcing him, but rather a gentle integration. I select the scene setting and propose to Claudio the selection of an instrument to represent the power of his group of roommates.

Session 19: Resources

Warm-up: I describe to Claudio what I have learned from reading the report the previous day, – about his aggressive behavior against his roommates. Claudio nods, but does not want to comment. He wants to act out the last weekend.

Play: Fishing with father.

Setting the scene: He plans the stage, – a blanket for the stream, two pillows, one for him, and one for his father. He chooses a Glockenspiel for himself and the metallophone for his father. A wonderful, peaceful scenery.

He says that the weekend was beautiful. With this beautiful **scene**, it is not easy to ask Claudio to also choose instruments for the other side, the events I saw in the report. He ignores my suggestion and wants to sit by the "stream" and wants to start the play. I stop him, "Stop! I know you from two sides. We are having a nice time here together, and you had a good time with your father last weekend. I'm happy about that. Yet, there is a reason why you are at the clinic. You have told me about the 'lump'." – Silence – "This seems to be a strong force which belongs to you too. – Put an instrument for this force onto the **stage**!" He immediately takes the conga and puts it on the edge of the stage and covers it with a cloth. He plays both **roles**, father and son, and then invites me to play the father using the metallophone. A soft flowing improvisation develops. We both enjoy the peace at the stream. At the end of the play he puts the conga away unused.

Feedback: "You have played a beautiful weekend with your father. You must be two people who enjoy peace and quiet." He agrees. "You did not use the conga." He does not want to comment.

Session 20: His own room

Warm-up: Playing the alphorn.

Play: Claudio would like to rearrange the room in the group home. I tell him to choose an instrument representing his "power in the group" which must certainly be important for his room with the group. He takes the conga, puts it at the edge of the stage and thinks. He does not want to act on the stage, but wants to draw the plan of his room with me at the table, in the audience area. Thereby the boundary problems and the quarrel with the roommates enter the conversation.

Feedback: "You took the conga and put it on the edge of the stage, without covering it." He shrugged his shoulders. "For your room you have thought of many things already which could be applied." (From the present objects, he has planned which ones he wants removed from his room, and instead of these he wants a stereo to listen to his music, undisturbed).

Process: Claudio has returned to a topic from the first sessions, namely to arranging his room. He has been at the clinic for a year now. I interpret his desire to arrange his living quarters as a sign that he is accepting the clinic as a neutral place, independent from both parents – a place he needs to gain clarity over his feelings, without standing in the constant solidarity conflict between his parents.

Session 21: The conga action

At the next session Claudio arrives and knows right away what he wants to play, "I'm playing the avenger!" The avenger takes revenge for acts against a woman who has been threatened, a story he saw on television. He plays the part of a TV hero. He goes on stage with the conga. He drums with all his strength. He chases away the evil people, supported by yelling: "Scat, you dog!"

Feedback: After the play, Claudio is glowing, hot and alive. He enjoyed the play a lot. I say, "The avenger is very scary! You played the conga very forcefully. What do you like best about the avenger?" "That they are all afraid of him, and that he is just!"

Process: Claudio chooses the conga as a power symbol for the just avenger. A part of his conflict is distinguishable. The lump is gaining shape. Claudio can approach his uncontrollable rage, embody and express it positively in the TV hero role. He experiences joy and satisfaction, and a good feeling of security when others are afraid of him.

Session 22: Breakthrough

Warm-up: In the next session, he just wants to listen; he says that he is so tired. He wants me to play the monochord. He lies in a cozy corner on the mattress and covers himself with the wool blanket. I give in to his wish (receptive music, psychic warming up, and nest warmth).

I play monochord with a constant beat. After a few minutes he gets teary eyed. Then he jumps up angrily and wants to step on the monochord and crush it. I quickly put the conga on the stage and secure the monochord.

Play: Claudio yells several times, "I'm going to kill her!" I ask, "Whom?" "Doris!" (Doris is the father's second wife). I say, "O. K., then let's play that!" I try to slow down the course a bit in order to set up a **scene** and to discuss the **roles**. The conga is already present. Claudio does not notice it. I take a blanket and put it on the rug (our stage), like a doll, and I ask, "Where is this?" – "In the forest!" says Claudio and starts stamping wildly on the blanket. He stamps his feet on the floor. On the soft rug (forest ground), his steps are barely audible. To support him, I take a djembe and accompany his stamping (**doubling**). I second his dynamics. His stamping is now audible. I am not sure what is going on inside him. He still stamps wildly on the blanket and yells every swearword that comes to mind and always repeats, "I'm killing you", then "Now she is dead!" He starts again, stamping a bit more slowly to turn her into mush, and have her disappear into the ground, as he puts it. Then he leaves the stage, sits down on the mattress and starts to weep. I sit down next to him. He cries for a long time and relaxes.

It is already past the hour, and the next patient is waiting at the door and knocks. I call out, "Please wait!" There is only time for a short discussion. Claudio says that since his grandfather's funeral he has never been as sad as now. He loved his paternal grandfather, who died three years ago, very much.

I give him **feedback** about the intense strength and anger he showed, and which I understood well, and tell him that anger and sadness were very close together today. I tell him this is often the case.

Process: In the preceding hour Claudio tested an intense hero-avenger-game with the conga. This time, he arrived at the session tired. Through a receptive **monochord warm**-up, his affects got stimulated (**psychic warm-up**), triggering strong anger against Doris. Does he want revenge for what happened to his mother? He kills Doris. It is beneficial to express anger with stamping since our legs are the strongest extremities. For reinforcement, I intentionally use a djembe and not the conga which remained available for him as a symbol of strength; perhaps he will need it later. He wants to make Doris disappear; she, whom he holds responsible for his father's adoption of her sons, and for not allowing him to say "father". After killing her, strong sadness emerges, with memories of mourning and loss of his grandfather. The lump is gaining more definition.

After the anger and the murder, relaxation and sadness followed, – a favorable integrative development. What will happen next weekend? From other sessions I know that he likes Doris quite well. She was a neighbor and he had often played with her sons. Therefore, I don't believe this woman to be in danger. When will he be able to see his idealized father more realistically?

Session 23 to the end of his therapy: Progress in full swing!

In the next session, after warming up with the alphorn, Claudio talks about the past weekend at Doris's home. He says that she is not always bad, and sometimes even quite nice. After this, his games are no longer so one-sided. He is now capable of being angry with his mother or father, and to also feel love for both of them. He is now better aware of "good and evil" parts in himself and in others, accepting them, and bringing them to the stage. From time to time, however, there are still attempts at dissociation, accusations, and bursts of anger, some highs and some lows. He is slowly acquiring an emotional balance.

In the last therapy phase, he is capable of recognizing and changing his own causative share in conflicts. Six months after the "stamping murder", the therapy is concluded, and Claudio is released to his mother with a good prognosis.

4.3 Reflections on the Contributions of Both Methods

In the previous example, music therapy and psychodrama complemented each other meaningfully. Without the music, this therapy would be as unthinkable as without psychodrama elements. The excerpts from this therapy were chosen to show the effect of the psychodramatic interventions. The music therapeutic parts are, however, equally important, showing clearly how the two methods are complementary and reinforce each other.

Music therapeutic areas of application

- Awareness and expression of feelings: Using the musical instruments Claudio was able to become aware of his feelings (8th session – alphorn, nightmare, 22nd session – monochord, receptive) and to make them audible (19th session – glockenspiel, metallophone – good feelings; 21st session – conga – murderous rage). These relieved him and gave the therapist the opportunity for targeted feedback (e. g., in the 19th session, dissociation of conflicts).

- Motivation: Strong motivation for the therapy came from the instruments and the music. The appeal of the alphorn was particularly strong for Claudio. He said repeatedly that he liked to come to make music, especially to play the alphorn.

- Physicality: With the alphorn he found better access to his body. He was able to control his breathing and speaking voice joyfully (2nd to 7th, 20th sessions).

- Resources: Through music Claudio always finds peace and creative energy. (19th session – duo with metallophone and glockenspiel – ability to enjoy; 20th session – warm-up with alphorn, – arranging his room).

- Nourishing and strengthening happened primarily in music therapy sequences, (duo with metallophone and xylophone and during sessions not described here).

- Relationship creation: By playing the monochord for Claudio, he felt secure (e. g., 22nd session). Improvisations with the metallophone and glockenspiel, as well as other improvisations without words, supported joyful relationship building and deep trust (9th–18th sessions). This allowed me to confront him later with the dissociation, without risking his breaking off our relationship.

- Holding and consolidation of experiences: Through musical accompaniment and taking up the dynamics (22nd session – accompaniment of his stamping) I showed Claudio my presence and my going along with him. In a later phase, I reinforced his experience with djembe beats.

doubling = Matching [handwritten margin note]

- Symbolization: From the first session on, the conga was a symbol of dangerous power (1st session – force which throws the lump; 19th and 20th sessions – symbol for rage with roommates); Claudio also chose the conga for the positive strength of the avenger (21st session).

- Catalyst function: The symbolic strength of the conga acquired a catalyst function (21st session) and allowed expression of anger up to his physical limits.

Psychodramatic spheres of action

- Access to suffering: The psychodrama work was best suited to gain access to Claudio's suffering. By dividing up the room, a creative picture of the pain (the heart with the lump) was created in the first session, and was observable from the audience.

- Awareness of the mental state: Through clear assignment of roles and the role exchange with the heart and the lump, Claudio was immediately able to portray his mental condition in a sensitive and differentiated manner (1st session). Through verbal doubling, unspoken feelings became conscious (feedback 1st session).

- Relief and reflection: The presentation of his problems with certain roles and role exchange expressed the fatalistic nature of suffering in an unburdening manner (1st session "the others threw me", 8th session "we have to do this"). With the room division, the patient was always able to be taken from his oppressive imagination or his dream to the secure audience area, or he could escape by himself and reflect while looking at the stage. Particularly with the work on the dream, and after the murder of the stepmother (21st session), this possibility was an important aid.

- Targeted work on the dissociation: With the scene setting it was possible to symbolize dissociated parts on the stage, and to slowly integrate them (conga on the stage, 19th, 20th, 21st sessions.)

- Sustainability and the promotion of awareness: With doubling it was possible to name things for which the patient had not yet found words, e. g., in the 1st session, the 'lump' crushes. During feedback, at the end of each session, the therapist had the opportunity to name the therapeutic accomplishment and to value it (1st session; 19th session). This helped the patient in accepting his difficult sides. The feedback motivated him to work on changes (20th session, arranging the room). Sustainability of the session was reinforced by verbal feedback. Awareness of the mixed-up description of the father was also helped by the feedback (8th session).

Transfer: Claudio often told the content of the feedback to his caregivers. This allowed them to encounter him with better understanding. I conclude from this that feedback helps the transfer from therapy to daily life. This was confirmed at the interdisciplinary meeting. Transfer from the group home to therapy was assisted by the stage setting (19th session).

5 Music Therapy with Psychodrama Session Structures

Music is an elusive medium, difficult to capture, even when we record it. The structural psychodrama elements enhance music therapy by making what would fade away more memorable, more concrete, and nameable. This synergy intensifies the therapy.

In particular, structured session design in three acts has been useful in music therapy: warming up – action/play – sharing/feedback. This structure gives patients support, as well as aiding awareness and memory. Session structure also helps the therapist, facilitating the recording of the session, grasp of processes, and report writing. Since there is often very little time in institutions for protocol writing and reflection, protocol forms prepared according to the session structure optimize these processes.

First, the three parts of the three-act sessions will be discussed and the protocol taking presented.

5.1 Session Design in Three Acts

Psychodrama sessions or session sequences are arranged in three parts or acts and start with a warm-up during which the topic of the session is established. The play/action phase is next which is then followed by sharing and feedback. It is very possible for a session to consist of multiple three-act components. I will describe the procedure for group therapy, which is also applicable to individual therapy. As soon as the group participants become familiar with the three-act structure, they are increasingly able to share about themselves and their problems during the warm-up. They know that at the end of this act, when the issues that have surfaced are taken up, they may comment or remain silent. Then they can decide what will be played.

In the play each member of the group has a role: protagonist, auxiliary role, or audience member. The participants, particularly the audience members, know that they will be asked during sharing about their own experiences, but they also know that they may remain silent. During the feedback round they can actively participate in the process of the protagonist with comments, and learn that their collaboration is helpful and valuable. This procedure usually requires an introductory phase. The separation of sharing and feedback is often difficult in the beginning.

As therapist, I am expected to lead the participants from one part to the next, and to decide with the protagonist whether or not an additional scene should be played, or if a sharing/feedback round should be next.

Like all rules and structures, these exist for the people we work with. When they are not useful, they have no intrinsic value and we can ignore them.

5.2 Warm-up

This phase was very important to Moreno, not only to establish a relationship and trust, but to support targeted processes, especially regarding roles. In music therapy "finding oneself" and "tuning into the therapy" are given careful attention. The gain from combining both methods is particularly clear in this phase. With musical interventions during the warm-up phase, with attention to the role categories, we gain new access to resources and to the suffering of patients. The warm-up based on role categories is therefore described in more detail in Chapter 6.

In individual therapy, the therapist takes up the topic with the patient and decides with him or her what will be played.

In group therapy, all topics are addressed by listing them or by setting up symbols. The group can then decide on the topic to be played. (See also in Chapter 12, Sociometry: choices).

5.3 The Play

Once the topic is chosen, the action phase can begin. The therapist decides if a group play (all participate in the chosen topic) or if a protagonist play is called for. First, the stage is set up.

Careful attention in this phase pays off later. Verbal exploration is often helpful. For a protagonist play, the protagonist should take ample time in choosing the instruments. In group therapy, the auxiliary actors are chosen during this phase.

When the instruments are set up, I ask, "Did we forget something important?" This provides the opportunity to point out missing, repressed or dissociated components, and gently bring them to the stage. In the previous case report, the dissociated anger was symbolized by the covered conga.

Once the play is planned, a scene is played musically, and if possible, without verbal interruption.

The task of the therapist is, based on her observations, to suggest a change of scene or end the play. In music therapy the change of scene corresponds to a new musical movement. The deliberate change of scene provides a wealth of possibilities, e. g., continue with the process, or suggest a new scene or a new musical movement, as described in Chapter 9 ("Scene change in Music Therapy"). With a **parallel situation**, the same topic in the family of origin, the present family, or at a different chronological age, a behavior pattern can be brought to awareness. With new **variations** we may, for example, expand flexibility, stimulate creativity, and develop a new meaning of life. Acting from different **perspectives** is often productive: How will it sound tomorrow, in a year, or in 10 years? It is incredible how much dormant strength and how many ideas can surface, and how they can lead to perspectives of the future. Often these also bring unsuitable fantasies to awareness.

If no new scene is announced, the play is ended by thanking all the participants for playing their roles. After removing the instruments from the stage, everyone meets on the audience chairs for the sharing/feedback round.

5.4 The Sharing/Feedback Round

Very few therapy methods work without feedback. Feedback is likely the most frequently adopted element from psychotherapy. In the following remarks, I will address the distinction between feedback and sharing because they have different psychodynamic and group dynamic effects and functions. I base my comments on the research by Reinhard Krüger (1998) adding my own experience from music therapy.

The sharing/feedback round is especially effective for adopting changes and for group cohesion. Things that might simply fade away are expressed in words, and sometimes with music. Both sharing and feedback can be expressed musically. However, for the transition from play to reality and to conclude the session, verbal feedback is usually better.

With groups, the sharing/feedback culture often needs to be developed. Both sharing and feedback are reactions to the preceding events. Sharing contains personal experiences which one is ready to share with others. For many it is hard to distinguish from feedback which contains responses to the actual play. Although sharing and feedback can never be fully separated, in sharing we focus on ourselves and contributions from the counterpart move to the background.

During sharing, our own contribution is in the foreground; during feedback, the focus is on the perception of others, and our own contribution, although still active, becomes background.

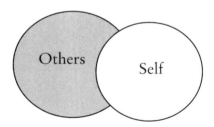

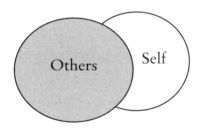

Sharing   Feedback

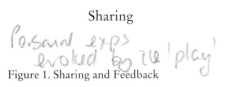

Figure 1. Sharing and Feedback

In both the therapeutic and the educational areas there are good reasons for using either sharing or feedback after a session. For example, there are individuals
who are "experts" at focusing the attention of the group on themselves by sharing,
putting themselves at the center and thus "robbing" the others. They always offer "much worse, much greater, more important" experiences. Plays listed under
"Plays for Sharing" are useful for integrating such individuals and giving them an
appropriate setting. It is, however, also possible to ask participants for feedback
only, thereby stimulating the awareness and perception of others. The different effects of sharing and feedback demand that the two types of interventions be considered separately.

Sharing

A play is usually followed first by sharing. The participants are encouraged to
share their own experiences, events from their own biography and feelings which
are echoed by the play. The group members as well as the therapist participate
in the sharing, in contrast to psychoanalysis which demands abstinence from the
therapist.

During sharing the therapist takes care of the protagonist who is now relieved
and may rest while the group members become personally involved.
Here are a few verbal examples for frequent sharing statements:

- I know this, I also had...

- I had a similar experience...

- In similar situations, I have the opposite experience...

- This reminded me of my aunt who is exactly the same...

There are also statements which do not show a clear connection to the member's
biography:

- I became so tired during the play. It was too much for me.
- I became so sad and I do not understand why.

Such statements deserve our special attention. They may point to preconscious
problems of the participants which can lead to emotional crises, even psychoses, if
suppressed. Such statements may also be based on transference or countertransference and are valuable. They should therefore be discussed again during the feedback round.

Effects and functions of sharing

- Promotes self-awareness

- Unburdens group members from pent-up feelings; afterwards, the feedback round is less tinged with consternation and responses are more accurate. In any case, one's consternation is apparent during sharing.

- Stimulates group members who are watching

- Reunites group after having played different roles

- Helps group members know each other

- Creates connection through problems. The protagonist finds out that he or she may have played his part as a substitute for someone else

- Supports acceptance

- Promotes individual processes in the group through identification with roles played on stage

- Can bring awareness of repressed feelings or events

Example from practice with a music therapy group: Sharing brings repressed emotions/events to light.

Irene, 48, is inhibited and fearful in teams. Her situation is characterized by failures and depressive moods. She attends a women's encounter group. For a group improvisation she chooses a kalimba, a soft-sounding instrument. Until now, she has always chosen a soft-sounding instrument, complaining kindly, and moralizing that in the group quiet, delicate individuals are not given any attention.

When someone values "always being kind", it is imperative to guide the expression of their aggressions. In the last session, I tried in vain with a change of scene.

Today, Irene complains again immediately after the play. I try to approach it during sharing and suggest that the actors who know Irene's situation and/or feelings present a sharing vignette from their own life. The following three vignettes have a strong effect on Irene, and she feels spoken to:

Sonja goes to the stage, sits down on a chair, lowers her head, and with a somber face, scratches on a tambourine. Title: "You are not allowed to be loud, it is not becoming for a girl."

Elvira also takes a tambourine, plunks down on the floor and rubs the hide with her fingers. Topic: "My brother already plays louder."

Renate takes the flexi-tone and holds it tight with both hands so that no sound can escape. She steps on the stage this way and returns to the audience. Her topic: "I have to be quiet, or my mother will get a headache."

Irene feels spoken to. The sharing shows her several possible causes for her 'belief system' that quiet is good and loud is bad.

During the next group session she chooses the djembe and plays "quarrel for two" with Sonja.

Irene never mentioned the origin of her being quiet, but her "having to be quiet" was gone. She developed healthy aggression and her depressed mood disappeared.

Play modes for sharing

1. Presenting vignettes

- Purpose: To embed the sharing topic into a situation and present it multi-sensorially, with gestures, musically and verbally, in order to remember it better. The therapist may suggest sharing vignettes for a salient topic in order to promote awareness.

- Procedure: Participants try to remember an episode from their lives, or imagine an episode fitting the proposed topic (like in the previous example from practice). They present this episode with instruments on the stage. They may also include additional participants. One vignette after the other is played, each concluded verbally with a title.

- Evaluation: New insights for plays, stimulated by the vignettes, are collected. The vignettes can provide the start of a new play.

2. Musical sharing (all in unison)

- Purpose: Emotional relief for participants allowing them to focus on the protagonist again. Stimulation of a group which is paralyzed by emotionality, or spellbound by the play.

- Procedure: Each participant takes an instrument or his/her voice and musically expresses his mood after the play, all members at the same time.

- Evaluation: The sound image which has faded away is named, preparing the transition to the feedback stage.

3. Verbal sharing

- Purpose: The participants' identifications become transparent. The protagonist finds out how he touched the participants and how well the topic he explored represented the group.

- Procedure: Free – anyone who wants to may comment. The protagonist listens.

- Evaluation: The topics that come up are collected.

4. Condensing the sharing using music and words

- Purpose: One's own feelings and memories are reflected on and concentrated into a topic. The effect of the play is remembered better and can be the warm-up for new plays.

- Procedure: All participants reflect on the effect the play had on them, perhaps it brought up memories of events or elicited emotions. All choose an instrument and improvise freely throughout the room, independent of each other. Participants who have found suitable music take a seat in the audience area. When everyone is ready, each member plays from his seat and briefly, in a word or sentence, presents his topic. With time limitations and large groups, it is also possible to just collect the individual topics, or have only a few people play music, since the process has taken place for all of them during the trial and reflection period.

- Evaluation: The therapist collects the topics.

Feedback

In everyday speech, feedback often means complaining or judging, but not in psychodrama. In psychodrama the intention is, "With my feedback, I am giving the other person a part of my observations as a present to make him feel recognized and appreciated. I give the other person something he does not yet see in himself." The feedback 'gift' may be accepted or rejected; the protagonist may state what type of feedback he wants.

If a protagonist does not want feedback, his wish is accepted. Resistance has a reason. It might be too much to take after a disturbing play, there may be fear of bullying, or there may be other reasons. Poor feedback culture opens the door to bullying. As a rule, bullying consists of no feedback or feedback that is wrong. Conversely, good feedback culture can help the positive development of the people involved, be it family, a school situation, or teaching. Everyone wishes to be judged kindly. However, feedback should not be adulation. This is worthless and a waste of time. If a trusting relationship is built, and a good feedback culture developed, then this phase is very effective for a good therapy process.

A good feedback culture is also effective in families, study groups and teams, not only in therapy. The ability to give and accept criticism is an important social skill.

Effects and functions of feedback

- Promotes respect and attention
- Supports self-esteem
  A series of improvisations in a session with feedback has a strong effect. In the form of the "Psychograms" developed by Katja Loos, a person plays himself with different facets and receives verbal feedback from the group. Then the next person plays or acts.
- Expands insight of participants
- Can reduce energy
- Can relax difficult group situations and provide security
- Can point out identification with the aggressor
- Helps in noticing changes
- Can establish relationships and expand social skills
- Can promote transfer from therapy to daily life

It is quite possible that after a round of feedback an additional play with its own round of feedback may follow.

Forms of play for feedback

As mentioned, feedback is a present which one may accept, reject politely, or secretly dispose of. Feedback is accepted with thanks and only exceptionally commented on. Since the actors feel to some extent similar to the people they portray, their feedback uncovers new feelings and understanding which were hidden from the protagonist.

1. Building feedback culture

- Purpose: The observation of others (modeling) is promoted. Feedback is understood as a present which is given to others and is not used as a weapon. Verbalizing of perceptions is practiced. Giving and taking are practiced.
- Organization:

  Giving:
- The therapist says where the audience and the players have to focus their attention. The participants give feedback on these points only.
- The participants examine their sympathy before they express feedback. If they don't feel supportive, and are annoyed, they can express this as an "I message" instead of feedback.
- The therapist oversees that feedback is not misused as bullying. Presents which contain "garbage" are returned! This is not only important in children's groups, but in other groups as well.
- The therapist may sometimes help in formulating feedback (wrapping the presents), to make them acceptable to the recipient.

Taking:

- The protagonist may specify for which points he desires feedback, and only receive and acknowledge a "feedback present" on these points.
- The protagonist states which presents he would like to keep, and which ones he cannot use at this time.
- All the participants who receive feedback practice examining it and setting it aside without comment, when necessary. If there is truly "garbage" in it, they should learn to reject it and, if appropriate, to complain at the right place, or draw constructive consequences and not "swallow garbage" – an important step for victims of bullying.

2. Role feedback

- Purpose: The protagonist learns from the role players about their feelings and situations in the play, and can gain new insight.

- Procedure: The protagonist poses questions to the role players and thanks them.

3. Audience feedback

- New insights or ideas for action.

- Procedure as above.

4. Applause

- Purpose: Thanking the protagonist and the players.

- Procedure: Clapping, voice or musical applause can reward a play before the sharing round, before the role feedback, or at the end. It may also be used to express joy and pleasure, and appreciation for a special effort.

5. The "Psychogram" by Katja Loos

Scene playing is performed to obtain feedback.

- Purpose: For the player: To be seen, to obtain new insight into oneself, to expand identity and self-image. For the audience: To practice awareness of others, to connect with metaphors, and to verbalize observations.

- Procedure: One person from the group gets up on the stage with one or several instruments and improvises on the theme: "This is the way I am." This is followed by the audience reporting their associations evoked by the play. These are written down and given to the player.

5.5 Protocols of Music Therapy Sessions with Three-act Psychodrama

To capture the sessions as efficiently as possible, I have designed the protocol forms according to the psychodrama meeting structure, and with additional psychodrama elements. Separately presented are:

• The group

• Date

• Title/topic

• Warm-up

• The names of the participants of closed groups are already on the form.

• After each session the different instruments and roles are entered next to the names.

• Sharing

• Feedback

• Session course

• Reflections on the process also contain thoughts for the next session.

The design of the form has worked well for everyday protocols. It provides easy overview of a group, facilitates recording group processes and processes of individual members, the planning of the next session, supervision, and report writing. Protocols of individual therapy are also simplified using these forms.

Group			Date [ ]	Session [ ]

Title	
Warm-up	

Name	Roles/Instruments	Sharing, Comments

Feedback	

Description	

Process	

Figure 2. Protocol Form for Group Therapy Sessions

Name   Date ☐ Session ☐

Topic Warm-up		

Name	Roles/Instruments	Sharing, Comments

Feedback

Description

Process

Fig. 3 Protocol Form for Individual Therapy Sessions

Protocols may be laid next to one another for analysis, to create reports, or for case controls in supervision. This facilitates the overview of the group process as well as the development of individual participants.

Group Q	1	Group Q	2	Group Q	3
Topic		Topic		Topic	
Warm-up		Warm-up		Warm-up	
Instr./Roles Sharing		Instr./Roles Sharing		Instr./Roles Sharing	
Patient A		Patient A		Patient A	
Patient B		Patient B		Patient B	
Patient C		Patient C		Patient C	
Patient D		Patient D		Patient D	
Patient E		Patient E		Patient E	
Patient F		Patient F		Patient F	
Feedback		Feedback		Feedback	
Course Description		Course Description		Course Description	
Reflection		Reflection		Reflection	

Fig. 4 Protocol Evaluation

6 "Warm-up" in Music Therapy
Based on Psychodramatic Role Theory

Warm-up in psychodrama is an energetic process similar to 'tuning' (German: *Einstimmung*) in music therapy. Tuning has many functions, such as making contact, transitioning from daily life to a therapy situation, and building energy. Schmoelz (1983, p. 59) writes that cautiously used, carefully adjusted modalities of musical tuning can result in an increased willingness by the patient to assimilate, act and process, thereby strengthening the effect of further musical therapy steps. In psychodrama, warm-up additionally stimulates certain targeted processes.

In the 90s, psychodrama research dealt intensively with these processes, focusing on what they stimulate and how one can control them.

In the following section I am going to use the term "warm-up" based on the psychodrama background rather than the general term "tuning". In the next paragraph, the energy sources involved will be discussed. Controlled musical warm-up at the somatic, psychological, social and transcendental levels will be introduced and followed by the corresponding forms of play. These are well suited for different settings, including group and individual therapy for children and adults, and also in part for educational settings. These are tested suggestions, mainly meant as examples to show a choice of warm-up approaches from one's own repertoire or from other sources, such as "Improvisation and Music Therapy" by Fritz Hegi (2010). Hegi has collected roughly 130 play ideas, many of which are suited for somatic and social warm-up.

The end of the chapter shows an overview table with music therapy warm-up examples according to Moreno's role classification. The functions and effects are assigned to four different levels: somatic, psychological, social, and transcendental.

What gets warmed up?

In everyday life we are exposed to constantly changing impulses in our relationships with other people, such as the forces of attraction and rejection. We are constantly confronted by new experiences and have to regain our equilibrium. These occur mostly without our awareness. Dreaming helps us with this. What cannot be processed is stored as tension. When we don't succeed in spontaneously settling these tensions, they act like magnets for associations and amplifications. Transferences may occur, and inner conflicts have an energy potential which urges us to action, to settlement (Dieckmann 1991). Moreno recognized this energy as a force for change and worked with it.

Krüger (1997) calls this energy "Überschussenergie" (excess energy). When we sense this energy, it can lead to re-orientation, i. e., to handle situations differently. He holds that if this energy does not proceed appropriately, it leads to crisis.

Depending on our ways of processing, we act differently in these crises and this leads to different pathologies. Depressed individuals tend to suppress impulses, hysterical individuals amplify them, neurotic individuals repress them, and schiz-oid types dissociate. Inadequate reactions, dysfunctional behavior patterns, and loss of energy follow. Spontaneity and creativity in everyday situations and inter-actions are suppressed.

By warming up we can get such excess energy back into swing and initiate the healing process. If only venting of energy takes place, tension reappears and even increases. In the warm-up process, excess energy grows and is used in the thera-peutic process. "Without pressure from suffering, there is no reason to change any-thing. Without excess energy, the energy needed for inner change is insufficient" (translated from German) (Krüger 1997, p. 49).

Through carefully chosen warm-up approaches, the necessary energy for the process is made available, and the patient is gently led to his topics. Changes and new orientations are strongly supported. Whenever possible, venting is avoided.

6.1 Somatic Warm-up

The goal of somatic warm-ups is to stimulate the energy of the participants. Breathing, circulation, movement, and self-awareness should become stimulated. The participants should focus on their well-being and get in touch with their own body. The perception of pulse, respiration, tension and movement is supported with music. In addition to building energy and body awareness, ambivalence, in-ner psychological conflicts, and individual issues can be stimulated through so-matic warm-ups.

Improvisations can also stimulate energy. However, they tend to lead to social awareness. Therefore, they will be mentioned under the topic of social warm-ups. If we want the participants to focus on themselves, they are less helpful.

Of course, it is possible that body exercises could stimulate topics from other role categories as soon as the energy level rises. A participant may arrive to group therapy with a "burning" issue. Even in this case, I would start with a somatic warm-up to increase energy levels which may be necessary for some participants. This way everyone is ready for action.

Example from practice with a children's music therapy group

A group of children with status D and B (maladjusted and cognitively weak) from two Swiss elementary school classes were referred to music therapy by the school psychologist. The four children, Berni, Fritz, Marc and Susanne, attend a weekly therapy session. They have usually had three hours of school before each session. Sometimes they already know what they want to play when they arrive. Today they are listless, sitting on the edge of the stage. To find energy, I suggest that someone play something (one of them or I) and that they move to the music if they feel like it. Berni wants to play. He chooses the lotus flute, which I have laid out among other instruments. We stretch up to his slow rising tone and sink down following the sound. I participate. The melody gets lively. The flute leads the movements. Our movements stimulate the player. His playing resembles that of a snake charmer. So we move like snakes. Berni's playing is fast and slow, loud and soft, all with the gliding sounds of the lotus flute. He is visibly happy that we are dancing to his flute. Upon my cue, he searches for an ending.

Now the listless attitude shown at the beginning of the session is gone. The children have not only come alive physically, they are full of ideas. Fritz and Marc want to play animals. Fritz says, "I want to be a tiger!" Marc also wants to be a tiger. Berni wants to be an animal researcher and Susanne wants to be a princess. The tigers want masks and no instruments, just their voices to roar. Quickly, masks are made from paper plates. The princess chooses a long dress from the props chest and a triangle. The animal researcher, Berni, takes a Boumhacker (a tuned plastic tube) as a telescope and we start.

Play synopsis: With loud roaring, the triangle playing princess gets attacked and eaten. Susanne then changes her role. She leaves the princess dress on the stage and becomes a tiger, too. ("Corpses" usually leave a piece of clothing behind and don't remain "dead" on the floor. They may join the spectators or pick a new role). Berni the researcher uses his Boumhacker to spot the animals and chases them. He catches a tiger and sells it at a high price to a circus. The other tigers also want to get caught and to be sold to the circus. Now that all the tigers are at the circus, the researcher also wants a job at the circus. He becomes a circus musician. The animals now dance to his music, roar, and practice stunts, which they all enjoy.

Role feedback: Fritz to Susanne, "I find it dumb that you always want to be a princess." Marc, "But it was fun to eat you." Susanne did not think that it was funny to be eaten. She thinks that playing tigers is 'dumb.' Therapist to Susanne, "But you continued to play right away as a tiger, and you liked it, or didn't you? You can play many other parts well, not only the princess with the triangle." Susanne laughs and is pleased. Therapist to Fritz, "You stole the princess; you were a dangerous tiger!" Therapist to Marc, "The circus paid a lot of money for you. You were happy about it. That was clear. In the circus you were very courageous and clever. The sensation of the show!" (He jumped from a chair through a wooden ring representing a ring of fire, onto a mattress.) Therapist to Berni, "You always found a role in order to be part of the action, twice with music. As the animal catcher you had many ideas. I was surprised that the tigers let themselves be caught and sold to the circus." Berni, "I was surprised, too. I thought they would run away and hide, and I would have to find them."

Process: By moving freely to the flute music the children regain energy. Individual issues get stimulated by the snake charmer music. Two boys, bursting with energy, choose physical roles. The two outsiders, Susanne and Berni, stay involved through role change. Berni is in contact with the group through music, being less successful verbally. With music and role choices, he even takes on a dominant role. The players are unaware of this. For them, the strongest or most expensive tiger is dominant. The fact of the sale to the circus is a surprising turn of the play. I would never have guessed that the two wild tigers would allow themselves to be caught in order to know how much they are worth, and that they would adapt and agree to be trained. They listened to the music of the circus director (not like in a real circus, where the music accompanies the animals). I am also surprised how Berni develops flexibility, from animal researcher to circus musician – he who often stands apart on the school playground and scarcely ever manages to join because he does not like to be wild. In music therapy, he cleverly picks roles which work for the play of others and allow him to be involved and creative. All three children reveal a lot about their values and ways of adjusting.

Figure 5. Tigers with Circus Musician at End of Play

Continuation: In the next session all four want to start playing circus right away, without warming up. Fritz, Marc and Susanne want to be tigers; Berni again wants to be an animal researcher. Tiger Fritz becomes deadly ill. He allows the others to take care of him. I am consulted as animal nurse. Berni, the animal researcher, travels to India to get a medication. He wants to save the tiger. Tiger Fritz is healed by the medication. For Berni this is a happy moment – for the tiger to accept the medication and to respond positively.

Play modes for somatic warm-up

Exercises for body awareness, following the music with movements, breathing and voice exercises, rhythm and body percussion, are all examples of somatic warm-up. It is important for each person to work by himself or possibly with one other person for massages, as explained below. In this case, one person "serves" the other person. If this ignites conflicts, it is better to avoid working with a partner, or to start right away with a social warm-up.

There are numerous somatic play modes which are also used in the pedagogic setting for energy building. In the music therapy literature, there are many descriptions; for children, e. g., in Lutz Hochreutner (2009, p. 200–215). More suited for adults are exercises from the play files of Fritz Hegi (p. 198, A1–A12, B1–B7 and R1–R7). I am including a few examples for illustration.

1. Movement to music

- Purpose: Through movement to music, respiration and circulation and thereby energy are playfully stimulated. Ambivalence may also be stimulated.

- Preparation: The therapist, a participant or a small group select instruments; they are the musicians. It is also possible to use an appropriate recording, but live music is better. The rest of the participants scatter around the room.

- Course of action: The music begins and the participants move freely around the room to the music, without paying attention to each other; they move as they feel at the moment. It is acceptable if connections occur.

- Evaluation: The therapist observes the group and may ask questions if she notices anything unusual. Then, one proceeds directly to a round of topic selection in which each participant can name a salient topic.

2. Foot flexion (exercise with partner)

- Purpose: Primarily to relax the back. This exercise can help in recovering energy after sitting or standing for a long time, after a strenuous day, for re-balancing and 'grounding.' It can activate inner conflicts. The play is centered on the recipient.

- Preparation: Blankets or mats, possibly pillows, and a musical instrument suited for pulsating, quiet music is chosen. (Moist washcloths and towels for foot washing may be provided.)

- Course of action: The participants work in pairs. One person lies down while the other kneels on a pillow or blanket at the feet of the first person, and puts the palms of his hands on the balls of his partner's feet, pushing lightly to the beat of the music. The therapist plays softly at a regular beat. It may also be pleasant for the person lying down to have the kneeling person place his fingers between their toes.

• Evaluation: Exchange about well-being and physical needs. Since this type of warm-up can be very relaxing, a second form of play with more motion is often effective.

3. "Purring Cat"

• Purpose: Body awareness, enjoyment of touch, relaxation and animation, stirring up of inner conflicts and uncertainties. The play is recipient oriented.

• Preparation: Blankets or mats, pillows, a musical instrument or recorded background music. The purpose of the music is to mask sounds uttered as well as for ambience in the room, like background music in a restaurant.

• Course of action: The participants work in pairs. Each pair takes a mat and a pillow. One person lies down on the mat, the other kneels on one side. The latter is the "giver" and thumps gently on the "recipient's" back. The recipient indicates with her voice (like a purring cat) what is pleasant and what is not. The giver then reacts or asks, if uncertain. The therapist or the CD player (in case of individual therapy) plays soft music. The givers thump on the receivers' backs until the music stops and then they change sides. During the next session, the roles are reversed.

• Evaluation: Exchange about mood and well-being.

Following a somatic warm-up, one can adopt a topic from the participants, perform an additional somatic warm-up play, or choose a warm-up play directed towards the process on a different level.

6.2 Psychological (Mental) Warm-up

A mental warm-up is often achieved listening to music. Many compositions, or the playing of the therapist, aim for an effect on the listener. Personal memories are most important for the intended effect. Personal episodes, the music connected to them and the energy they contain, are all stimulated; affects and moods can be enhanced and changed. Music provides space and time in which feelings can flow.

Example from practice: mental warm-up of a member of a music therapy encounter group.

Rolf, 44 years old, is a member of an encounter group (3 men and 9 women, a one-week course). He enjoys playing, but shares little. After the morning session on the third day he comes to see me, and asks to make use of my offer of a private office visit. (A psychoanalyst and I work together and offer participants an office visit.)

Mental warm-up: He finds that the course does not bring him what he had hoped for. "I am feeling progressively worse. If I only knew why I always get sadder when I hear or play music." I had noticed Rolf's sadness during the sessions. I ask him if it happens only in this course. He says no, and mentions that there is a piece of music that always makes him cry, and therefore he does not listen to it any more. "Bach's Air is very bad. I get so sad and afraid; an enormous, incomprehensible fear." I find this reaction unusual for this piece which is rather consoling, and which I have played as a cellist at many funerals. This piece of music could be a key to a repressed trauma. I suggest that Rolf bring this piece to the afternoon session. He absolutely refuses. However, he is willing to listen to it with me. That much he would risk. After discussing it with my colleague, I accept. He is afraid, but also somewhat curious. We sit down back to back in the music room and listen to the original orchestra version of the work. As the piece ends, Rolf starts sobbing, whimpering, and then soon starts crying loudly; it flows like a stream out of him. We are still sitting back to back. After a while I begin to move slightly from side to side. His crying quiets down and he lets himself be led and is relaxed. Then he begins to talk, "My father…" I wait for minutes. "The funeral of my father! They played this piece – it has been eight years, and I was glad that he had died." Now we know the wound.

Course of action: In the next group session he talks about his experience with the Bach "Air". Now he is able to bring a scene from childhood to the stage with music, a situation from childhood with his father who teased him, locked him up, and laughed about his fears. He chooses a small drum for himself, a large one for his father, and a group member to play him. When the father plays loud and hard, he becomes silent. When I stand next to him, his anger rises and he can beat the drum loudly; when I move away, he is overcome with paralyzing fear. His feelings of abandonment are so paralyzing that he can no longer feel his anger, unless I stand next to him. Then the fear vanishes, his strength returns, and the anger rises. In this scene he says he does not feel any sadness, only anger and fear.

Sharing and feedback: When the participants share his anger in the sharing and feedback round, the sadness surfaces again, which he now allows himself to feel. Many participants who have had similar childhood experiences share with him. He now allows himself to show feelings in the group and feels support. The ice is broken, without him drowning in feelings.

Process: Rolf had signed up for the one-week course because he felt overwhelmed with everyday life. The two previous days in music therapy with the group, experiencing the stories of the other members, did not bring him the expected relaxation and recovery, but activated the excess energy from his father problems. The "musical conserve Bach Air" that he listened to in the one-on-one session led to memory traces and brought up the excess energy from the father problem. The physical closeness, being back to back, led him to allow the surfacing of bottled sadness which he could not allow himself to experience before. It was sadness for the father whom he missed, the inner father who he would like to have had. The anger at the dead father and the feeling of liberation at the funeral were apparently the whole truth.

During play with the group, Rolf experienced his intense anger against his father once more, mixed with fear of abandonment, and during feedback, once more, the sadness. The one-on-one situation and the sharing in the group helped him overcome his fear of abandonment.

Rolf can now express anger, sadness and fear, and is no longer blocked emotionally. He dares to show feelings in a group. An encounter with the dead father is now possible. This enabled a first step towards integration of the topic.

Play modes for mental warm-up

Several forms of receptive music therapy are suitable for the mental warm-up step. The therapist plays or a participant plays, or recorded music is played. Although people react differently to music, it is possible to adapt the music to the mood of a group or to support relaxation, or to stir the emotional experience with a musical voyage. Music is always feeling-oriented and touching even when it annoys some people, bores some, and moves some to tears.

Relaxation is a good prerequisite for mental warming up. Feelings are more noticeable in a relaxed state. But relaxation does not always have the expected effect. We learn this during sharing. This was the response of a group of 12 female and 4 male participants after 15 minutes of monochord play: 9 female and 3 male participants found the sound very pleasant, relaxing and of the right length. One female participant got a headache, for another it was too short to relax, and one fell asleep; for one male participant it was too long and he became restless. So for three of them, it failed to be relaxing!

Relaxation reduces control over feelings. With traumatized individuals – and we often don't know that they are traumatized – flashbacks may occur. With the monochord sound for example, old memories of hiding in air shelters with bombers flying overhead were recalled, and led to fear and panic. From men who at the end of the monochord play manifested fear and panic, I learned that their mothers had been very depressed during or after their pregnancies. Other floods of feelings occurred as well. Such reactions may be useful diagnostically for further process with the group, but can be dangerous for pre-psychotic individuals. Flashbacks should be avoided by all means, and keen attention by the therapist is required!

Mental warm-ups are important in the educational setting when the goal is to stimulate associations with a topic, such as in school at the beginning of art or composition class.

1. Relaxation with the monochord

• Purpose: Relaxation, flow of feelings, stimulation of personal topics.

• Preparation: The participants take mats and the therapist prepares instruments.

• Course of action: Participants scatter in the room and are helped to relax. The therapist plays different gently augmenting and diminishing notes with different harmonics/overtones, and observes the breathing and other movements of the participants. When they become restless, the play is terminated. The participants are given time to become aware of their mood and to come back to the "here and now".

• Evaluation: The experience of listening is shared. Several possibilities are available for this purpose
  – The therapist can test the mood with specific questions
  – The participants can share freely about their experience
  – They can share in small groups
  – They can bring their experience "to the point" and choose a title for it
  – They can choose an instrument and play to express the mood to the group (1 min).
  – They can all play at the same time, but each to himself, then find a title for their experience

2. Musical requests and "famous melodies"

• Purpose: Episodes connected with the sounds are recalled. In geriatrics, geriatric psychiatry, and with refugees, this form is of great value. With a love song from the youth of an individual, a song from the country of origin, or with a requested piece, the participants are led to their personal memories. Memories of traumatic experiences are possible and caution is advised.

• Preparation: Comfortable chairs (or better, padded chairs with armrests) and suitable music (instruments or recorded music).

• Course of action: Participants sit comfortably and if possible, close their eyes; they are encouraged to relax. Music is played. If physical closeness represents security for patients, closeness can contribute to relaxation and bring access to new feelings, as in the preceding example from practice: "Mental warm-up by a member of a music therapy encounter group".

- Evaluation: Personal, beautiful or difficult memories can be shared and can be better integrated by talking about them. Protagonist plays become possible.

3. "Sound Journey"

- Purpose: Alternating sound experiences lead the listener to different inner voices and images. Associations with the sounds are stimulated. Individual themes are stimulated. Episodes associated with sounds are evoked (guided imagination).

- Preparation: The therapist develops, based on the preceding session protocols or her goal for the group, a "sound voyage", a sequence of musical motifs with one or more instruments.

- Course of action: The participants lie or sit in comfortable positions and are helped to relax by the therapist. This is followed by the musical sound journey.

- Evaluation: There are several ways to capture the topics which have surfaced and to "preserve" them for the next sessions:
- Each participant chooses a title for the sound journey and the therapist writes them down.
- Each participant draws his sound journey.
- 3–4 people trade and then report in the plenum.

6.3 Social Warm-up

A social warm-up serves to help group members get acquainted, and to help integrate new group members or outsiders within the group. It also stimulates social experiences and transferences. Actual interpersonal problems within a group can become apparent. The following example shows a warm-up used to increase familiarity within a group and the members' ability to work together.

Example from practice of social warm-up at the beginning of a workshop at an international congress

Preparation: My task is to convey and discuss music therapy methods in 1 ¾ hours. The participants are professors, therapists and students from all the European countries; the language is English, a foreign language for almost all participants. As quickly as possible, the most varied role carriers have to take on the role of workshop participant and make contacts among themselves (30 participants). An emotional awareness and security has to be won in order to allow all of them to work together and to have open discussions.

Warm-up: Small musical instruments and items from the cafeteria such as spoons, glasses, chrome plates – items with which noise and sounds can be produced – are lying around the room. As they enter the room, some participants already get busy with the instruments. The appeal of the instruments and the participants' curiosity are enormous. To take advantage of this energy and to avoid a long round of introductions which could lead to posturing due to the amount of rational and verbal power in the room, I suggest that they choose an instrument (or two) and try to make brief musical contact with each participant. "As soon as you have greeted everyone this way, put the instruments back and sit down, all without talking. You have 10 minutes; after that I'll end the exercise with a sound signal."

After the exercise we remain quiet for a moment. Then I encourage the participants to re-member, with whom did I make eye contact? With whom was it pleasant? With whom was it difficult? About whom would I like to know more? At this point, the round of verbal introductions begins. It is short, to the point, and personal. All are quick to make contact and the group is ready to work together.

Feedback: "Never before have I had such personal contact with students!" "Wonderful, that professors are playful people too!" "Amazing how quickly one can make contact with music!" "This was fun and removed all the achievement and presentation pressure!"

Process: Working together started with a common experience. At this point the participants were all the same. The differences in education, rank and age moved to the background. A long verbal introduction could have created barriers among this mixed group of partici-pants. All had an emotional basis for participating in the workshop. The psychodramatic preliminary considerations proved successful.

In this musical "one-on-one", tensions could have surfaced. In that case, I would have encountered them on this level right at the beginning, adjusted my offer, and improved familiarity with sociometric means, exposing the tension, which could otherwise have blocked the work. Exposed tensions are less disturbing for social life than hidden ones.

Play modes for social warm-up

For social warm-up, I distinguish different aspects:
- formation of groups
- promotion of familiarity and trust in the group
- competition and conflicts
- self-awareness and awareness of others
- security in the group
- relationship and communication.

Many forms of improvisation are suitable, as described by Fritz Hegi (2010) among others.

Sociometric exercises for group building and promotion of familiarity in groups are described in Chapter 12 (Sociometry).

Play modes for group formation:

1. "One-on-one" with each participant

- Purpose: Closeness is facilitated in the group. Conflicts can arise and old relationship experiences may be triggered.

- Preparation: A selection of small instruments is set up. They should be easily playable while walking around. The voice may be used. However, no talking!

- Course of action: Each participant chooses an instrument and contacts someone else with it. A small duet is played after which one leaves and moves on to the next person. When everyone has been greeted musically, they sit down in the spectator area.

- Evaluation: A short feedback session, like in the preceding example from practice, may be sufficient. Through the questions asked by the therapist, behavior patterns can become apparent: How do I make contact? Do I wait to be spoken to? Do I search for eye contact? Do I react to rhythms or more to sound or melody? Who usually leaves first? May I leave, or do I wait for the other person to leave? Did I notice a dominant pattern for myself? These questions can also be asked as a self-awareness task at the beginning of the play.

2. Competition in groups

- Purpose: To allow competition and to enjoy competing. To uncover competition and deal with it.

- Course of action: Two or more subgroups are formed. They face each other with instruments and challenge each other with the instruments or with their voices. They try to dominate, to set the pace, and to win over the members of the opposing group. Which group can keep its beat the longest? Which group gives up? Which one persists?

- Evaluation: Sharing/feedback round

3. "Dueling" groups

- Purpose: To fight, to face competition by a group, to assume a position in the group, to win and lose and to preserve one's respect in front of the opponent and express it.

- Course of action: Two (or more) subgroups are given competition tasks: the competition takes place as a duet (duel), i. e., each subgroup chooses a member and sends him or her to the stage where the competition takes place. The competition can be who can hold a note longer (voice or instrumental), or two people, each with a tambourine and drumstick face each other, and the number of beats are counted, etc.

- Evaluation: In the sharing/feedback round, mutually congratulatory feedback is exchanged by winners and losers. The question, "How were the presenters chosen?" is answered.

4. Musical "Sociodrama"

This form of play may also be used in education, in team development and in group studies.

- Purpose: Through musical expression of different aspects of a conflict, new approaches can emerge. Through role exchange, all participants experience the different positions in a conflict. Empathy can develop and compromise becomes possible. In psychodrama this approach is called "sociodrama".

- Course of action: A problem that surfaces in the group is dissected on the stage into different opinion positions, personal positions or other aspects, and presented musically (e. g., opponents, neutral individuals; students, teachers, parents; early risers and late risers; fussy ones and sloppy ones, etc.). This way it becomes more transparent for all. Now the therapist lets the group build "parties" which take on different positions. These groups pick instruments, present their positions or aspects musically and name them verbally.

  Then role exchange takes place. Group A plays from the position of Group B with the instruments of Group B; Group B takes position C and Group C takes position A – until each group has played all the positions.

- Evaluation: Sharing/feedback, formulation of solution approaches, collection of personal topics.

5. The "Problem"

The "problem" represents a difficulty which appears in the group or which affects the group. The problem is turned into an object through symbolization. It is turned from a personal problem into one "owned" by the group.

   This form of play may also be used in supervision. In case supervision, this allows for collecting "problems", choosing topics, and possibly starting to work on them.

- Purpose: The problem is to be presented openly, symbolically and musically, in order to clarify whether it belongs to a participant or the leader, or if the problem is a scapegoat phenomenon or has institutional roots, etc. As a symbol, initially detached from individuals, it can be examined from all sides. It should become apparent whom it concerns. The playful approach should encourage creativity and energy towards solving the problem, promoting acceptance, and possibly leading to a protagonist play. It can also lead to relationship discussion, improve the working ability of the group, or stimulate a further step in the group process.

- Course of action: The problem is presented. If there is an accuser/plaintiff, she can place an instrument on the stage and play it the way she sees the problem. If there is no plaintiff, the therapist can name the problem and place an instrument in the center. Different aspects may be presented symbolically with instruments. The therapist suggests further interventions for working on the problem, e. g.,

  - While the plaintiff plays the problem instrument, all the group members get on stage with the problem. That is, they choose a position on the stage that, in their opinion, corresponds to the right distance and posture. They can participate in the improvisation with their voices or with instruments.
  - All participants who know the problem play the problem instrument, one after the other, and then remain on the stage.
  - All participants who know the problem form a chorus and sing, rap or chant.
  - All participants who know the problem from different situations (outside the group) play the problem instrument one after the other, or choose a different instrument and join the people on stage.
  - Everyone who has a problem related to the group chooses an instrument, places it on the stage and plays it.
  - Participants who see a solution, present it.
  - Anyone who disagrees can express his position with an instrument.
  - Negative spirals can be approached with humor and/or reinforcement.

- Evaluation: Usually the stimulated energy and the topics that have surfaced are enough of a warm-up for a single intervention. Depending on the problem, role exchange is also advisable here.

6. The "Mirror Circle"

- Purpose: To develop better awareness of oneself and others, notice impulses from oneself and others, and expand self-image. To develop confidence in the group and possibly expose bullying.

- Course of action: Group members choose an instrument to introduce themselves, or a play to reflect the current mood, and form a circle.

  - A participant goes (or jumps, dances) to the center of the circle and plays/ names/calls out/sings his name.
  - He returns to the circle and remains there, observing the group.
  - Each of other participants now goes to the center and imitates the observed performance with his body and instrument as precisely as possible, and then returns to the circle.
  - This is repeated until everyone has performed.
  - If 'aping' or distorted presentations occur, the therapist demands more careful observation by the group.

- Evaluation: Collection of topics

During warm-up for relationship or communication problems, many forms of improvisation without psychodramatic elements are suitable. Sociometric exercises are also well-suited for social warm-ups. Several of them are listed in Chapter 12, "Sociometry in Music Therapy".

6.4 Transcendental Warm-up

Psychodrama would like to address all phenomena of human behavior. This includes "transpersonal roles", or the supra-individual being. Transcendence in psychodrama is not a religious concept; it is closer to Sartre's definition. For Sartre (1997), transcendence was the "exceeding of the ego", and an ever-present connection with the cosmos. It is the connection to everything that surrounds and encompasses us.

The transcendental role level in psychodrama also goes further than ethics, which is more related to the social level.

To stimulate roles on the transcendental level, various methods of warming up can be used: rituals, meditative dances, work with pictures, fairy tales and myths, poems, contemplative and provocative texts. These stimulate at the sensory level. Transpersonal themes and energy for creating new perspectives can be stimulated, opening up access to one's spirituality. A deep sense of connection with the world can be felt. Reconciliation with one's fate and integration of losses can be promoted.

Rituals are a good way to access this area. Research on rituals has shown that humans as well as animals need rituals for security and to effect control. Through rituals, we recognize "friend and foe". Repetition of rituals results in security and familiarity. It has been claimed that the basis for rituals is "psychosomatic", i. e., they have a physical basis (posture, movement) and an emotional basis (Bellinger/Krieger 2003). For music therapeutic rituals this suggests that the inclusion of rhythm and sound elements that have a stable, repetitive form is best. Ostinati are particularly well suited. Ostinato, which is a regular, repetitive musical motif, is found in many styles of music – it is basically a harmonic sequence, in jazz and rock a "riff". Ostinato provides security and forms the basis for melody and improvisation. Among the most-played orchestral works are the Pachelbel Canon and Ravel's Bolero. In the Canon, the bass plays an ostinato from beginning to end, a harmonic motif of eight notes, while the higher strings play variations. In Ravel's Bolero two drums play the ostinato, a continuous rhythmic motif above which the orchestra plays variations. Ostinati can "rock" and "carry", "penetrate", "swing", "wind up" and "soothe". Ostinato is versatile and effective with its persistent repetition.

In my studies at the C. G. Jung Institute I dealt intensively with pictures, fairy tales, symbols and associations during therapy. Therefore I often use pictures and fairy tales in the transcendental warm-up as a basis for improvisation. Fairy tales connect us to transcendental "prototype roles", the archetypes. The texts and pictures stimulate associations, and the music enhances feelings. With an actual picture, which may also be looked at after playing the music, a transient musical picture can be remembered better.

Two examples from practice are shown below to demonstrate transcendental warm-up. The first example is about finding meaning in a fairy tale. In the second example, there is a group improvisation to a photograph, which stimulates perspectives and motivation.

Example from practice for transcendental warm-up with a children's music therapy group

The children were referred to music therapy from the school psychology service due to behavior problems.

Warm-up: The new group starts the first session with, "The Town Musicians of Bremen" (German: *Die Bremer Stadtmusikanten*). I tell the story which they already know from kindergarten. Every time an animal is mentioned, we 'play' it with our voices. All of the children play the donkey, the dog, the cat and the rooster once. It results in four spooky but beautiful concerts with different vocal ranges.

The play: After this practice in transcendental roles, we play the fairy tale freely. The four rejected animals find each other. All the unwanted animals, exposed to misery, decide to stick together to have a better life. They rest in the forest. The donkey and the dog lie under a tree (a table), the cat sits above them (on the table), and on the top (a chair on the table) stands the rooster; all sing at the top of their lungs. They cooperate; the group is born, connected by the common play and their own (common) misery.

Process: This fairy tale contains Moreno's role categories. The donkey is an old image for the body (somatic role); the dog, the most faithful companion, with instinct and sensibility, stands for the mental/psychological role; the cat, a symbol for the vagabond. In ancient Egypt the cat is the symbol for Bastet, the Goddess of Protection for mothers and children (transcendent role). All four characters play together. They harmonize, get strong together and transform the robber's house into a residence (Hofer-Werner 1998). Is there a more fitting picture for a music therapy group of children with behavior problems and who have been expelled from the regular classroom? I love this fairy tale and the children love it, too. This transcendental warm-up was the beginning of a therapeutic role development: to get along better with friends.

Example from practice: transcendental warm-up with a group of adults

My task is to lead an encounter and methods training group for music therapy students. The participants are 15 students at the end of their 6th semester, in the last week before semester break. After the break, some of them will enter practical work under supervision, do research, or write their Master's thesis. This session is about their identities as therapists.

On the wall of the music therapy center there are many souvenir photographs from the training program, and also pictures of students in the 8th semester who took their Master's final exam three weeks earlier. I suggest that they look at the pictures on the wall and let them 'sink in'. Then they are to choose one or more pictures and set them to music. The students agree immediately, choosing the following picture: the entrance to the university – stairs and a door, framed by impressive columns. On the steps, the freshly graduated music therapy Masters stand with bouquets of flowers in their hands.

The students can choose which elements they want to adapt for voice and movement to music. Three students volunteer right away to portray the columns and two the steps. They get on stage. The steps portrayers sing the first five notes of a major scale evenly up and down. The three column portrayers sing the root and fifth an octave lower, holding the notes.

Now the actors who portray the newly graduated Masters get between the stair portrayers and column portrayers and a flower bouquet portrayer stands next to each of them. One student chooses to play the shadow, which she plays with a permanent hissing sound. On the picture it is a sunny day with strong shadows. Her motto, "No light without shadows".

The steps sing their five notes up and down regularly, the columns hold a fifth continuously and the Masters jubilate. The flower portrayers sing delicate, repetitive flourishes. It creates a wonderful sound image. After a while the Masters and flowers leave the stage and become silent. The steps, the columns, and the shadow remain on stage; a standing fifth with the regular intervals, don, don, don, don, don; the shadow, shshsh; all are almost 100 years old, standing and lasting, ready for the next Masters, who will hopefully be this group of students. All are deeply touched by this spontaneous, impressive improvisation.

Figure 6. The University Entrance Awaits the New Music Therapy Masters

Feedback: The students call the warm-up gratifying, motivating, identity promoting, focusing on the profession. They particularly liked the effect of the simple, clear, sustained harmony as a calming influence next to the active jubilating, and the decorative flowers, resulting in a pleasant, stimulating force field. They mention during role feedback that the 'Master players' felt in this rejoicing moment that they were anticipating their own selves standing there someday. This gave them strength, an inner fire. For others, the crucial moment was when nobody was left on the steps. This provoked a feeling of, "Now it is our turn!" During sharing, several students said that during the play they made the decision to also be there in a year. I mention that I am in a similar situation, on the way to these steps. Two students who are over forty and who were afraid of being too old, feel encouraged by my sharing.

Following this beginning of a three-day seminar, intensive plays about the identity of music therapists were facilitated. Transcendental warm-up provided a motivating, meaningful start. The energy lasted to the end of the seminar.

Play modes for transcendental warm-up

1. Breath and voice

- Purpose: The participants make contact with each other through breathing and voice. The common air, the common room and the common sound connect and surround. A sense of community, security and trust ensues.

- Procedure: The beginning is similar to a somatic warm-up with the difference that we are arranged in a circle (not scattered around the room) and we look at each other. The distance between participants reflects the familiarity of the group. Holding hands or holding the shoulder of the next person may be appropriate.
  - Quiet – looking around the circle and breathing slowly
  - Humming
  - Perhaps the circle starts walking
  - Solo parts are possible
  - Moving apart by walking away singing or subsequent quiet opening of the circle in order to bring the feeling into the spectator space.

This mode of play can also be used as farewell ritual.

2. Ostinato with voice

The following group exercise was first experienced with Fritz Hegi.

- Purpose: Regular ostinato singing can support the feeling of security and community, enhance concentration, and through the constant repetition (depending on ostinato) strengthen a voice. As a result, topics are stimulated at the transcendental level.

- Procedure: Stand or sit in a circle. The therapist or a participant sings an ostinato for the group until the group can join in. The physical demands of the ostinato should be such that it can be sustained for a long time.

- As soon as the group can sing the ostinato steadily, individual participants may break out from the ostinato and sing a solo.

This type of play may also be used as a closing ritual.

- Evaluation: Topics that surfaced are collected.

3. Rhythmic ostinato

- Purpose: With a sustained rhythm that fits the mood, a group can be animated or calmed down. If a group plays a common pulse, the pulse frequency may slowly be adjusted. A meditative mood can be created. Transcendental topics can be stimulated.

- Procedure: A rhythm is presented and the group plays along synchronously. Participants may also take turns playing solos. It can be performed as a drum circle.

- Evaluation: Suggested topics are collected.

4. The ornament

- Purpose: Each individual contributes to the whole. With constant repetition, musical phrases become supportive. Where initial thinking and counting is required, eventually one feels carried by the music. Self esteem and presence in the group without dissolution is being practiced. A "we" feeling is created.

- Process: The participants take an instrument and rehearse a musical phrase that they can repeat many times. One person starts playing. One after the other joins in and fits his phrase (1–4 sounds) into the ornament, repeating it as evenly as possible. The group plays until all the participants know the structure of the ornament so well that they can stop thinking and counting and let themselves be rocked by the ornament.

Figure. 7. Ornament by Regula Mitchell

5. Circles dances

- Purpose: The group moves synchronously. The activity of the individuals becomes tied to and subordinated into a common form. Unburdening from responsibility, being carried, reduction of pain, and the will to live may all be stimulated, but also fear of dropping out of the group, failing to fit in, and fear of self-dissolution can occur.

- Preparation: The therapist needs to prepare well, both musically and with planning. If no assistant if available (musician or dancer), one has to use CDs or prepare a simple mood-appropriate musical motif for singing repetitively with the group, to which they can walk or dance. Whoever does not care to compose their own, may use folk songs, Klezmer melodies, etc. Have water available! Singing and moving makes you thirsty!

- Procedure: With inexperienced groups it is better to introduce them first to the music, to sing and then walk in a circle. This is also suitable for children's groups. The physical closeness, perhaps holding hands or shoulders, has to fit the nature of the group. Dancing is performed, if possible, until a flowing group motion is created.

- Evaluation: No immediate evaluation, as a rule; however taking a break and drinking are recommended. Then further work with the stimulated topics.

6. Rituals and songs for beginning and ending

- Purpose: To create togetherness, closeness and openness in the group; to offer safety through clear structure. Through the ritual, associated with pleasant memories, positive expectations are prompted, and transition to the work is facilitated.

  Starting rituals are particularly helpful with groups that do not meet weekly, or in geriatrics with forgetful or demented individuals. Listening to repetitive music, instant recall often occurs, without need for explanation, reminding them that they are in music therapy. Introductory songs and other greeting rituals build trust, lift the spirits and evoke positive expectations.

- Preparation: For children's groups, develop simple greeting and goodbye rituals, e. g., a starting song or a greeting ritual. Literature on music therapy and pedagogy offers many additional suggestions.

- Procedure: Introduce and maintain a beginning and ending ritual. These may be a song, the singing greeting of each individual person with name, the common listening to a certain sound or another steadily repeatable form.

Warm-up rituals often start before therapy. For instance, it makes a difference whether patients arrive well combed and groomed for therapy or whether they are hastily shuffled away from their coffee, with jam on their fingers, by overworked personnel. These transition rituals could possibly be modified as well; it is beneficial to take care of these situations.

7. Music in association with pictures

- Purpose: Pictures stimulate participants to make associations, to put these associations to music and to create a symbolic musical image. Creative connections occur, which usually results in focusing of the group energy. It can empower the group to face difficult topics and difficult protagonist plays. Topics dealing with life perspectives and the meaning of life are stimulated. If there are acute problems on the social level, these can also be stimulated by group work with pictures.

- Preparation: Pictures (photos or paintings) with people, landscapes, buildings, humans and animals, weather conditions, special events, celebrations, ceremonies, etc. are suitable. The therapist assembles an assortment appropriate for the group.

- Procedure: The group selects a picture. Each participant chooses an element in the picture or a place within it to which she wants to play music. A picture of a farm can lead to topics for plays, such as security, the smell of manure, the sound of mice in the wall, cows in the barn, memories of time spent on a farm, childhood, vacations with grandparents, the roof, the fireplace, the entry stairs, the tree in front, the cat on the stairs, the laundry on the clothesline, fear of the dog, etc. The picture is placed on the stage and enacted. Should the associations be very personal and dramatic, then the next variation, "Suite to the picture", can be played.

- Evaluation: Sharing, listing of topics.

8. Suite to the picture

Purpose and preparation are the same as for Exercise 5. The therapist may choose more "dramatic" pictures in order to stimulate suspected topics.

- Procedure: The picture is selected by the group (perhaps sociometrically). Each person chooses an element in the picture, names it, takes an instrument and goes on stage. Then the sequence of the musical suite is determined and played in order.

- Evaluation: Listing of topics and possibly a sharing/feedback round.

9. "Pictures of an Exhibition"

- Purpose: Same as for Exercise 5. This exercise is also suitable for enhancing familiarity in the group and with the available instruments. It is also possible to stimulate topics on the social level.

- Procedure: Several pictures are chosen with themes, feelings, seasons, moods. The pictures are placed on the stage. The subgroups play musical phrases to the pictures in sequence.

- Evaluation: In this exercise, a feedback round by the audience is fruitful.

10. "My Music to My Picture"

• Purpose: With each person having to choose his own picture, an instrument and solo play, several personal decisions have to be made. This strengthens identity. Through musical expression and compassionate listening by the therapist and group members, the feelings of the player are intensified, and energy for change or enforcement of resources stimulated. Often the self-image becomes more nuanced.

• Procedure: Each person chooses a picture and prepares a short play. The pictures are shown in sequence; the topic is announced and played with music. The order may vary.

• Evaluation: Topics, most often about the way of life, are collected for further work. Sharing and feedback can be productive for plays.

11. Fairy tale music

• Purpose: Identification with archetypes of humanity, which appear as symbols for the human experience in fairy tales, myths and legends, is stimulated. The sense of connection with people from primeval times who had similar fates can stimulate topics on the meaning of life, acceptance of misfortune, etc., and bring courage for facing new aspects.

• Preparation: The therapist looks for a fairy tale as a metaphor for the group situation or for the situations of individual group members, in order to get everyone involved in the topic.

• Process: The story is told or read.
  – Each person chooses a character that touches them and which they wish to play; this may also be an animal, a plant, or an object. Characters may be played by more than one cast member, be presented as a choir, or form an instrumental range of sounds.
  – The group decides together which scene will be played, or at least which scene will be played first.
  – Each person chooses an instrument (or voice) and starts warming up.
  – Then the scene gets set up on the stage. Each person looks for a starting point.
  – The start and finish are marked by a cue from the therapist. A player who wants to quit or leave his role, puts his instrument away and goes to the spectator area. Individuals who "die" or "are killed" leave their instrument on the stage and also move to the spectator area.

• Evaluation: Listing of stimulated topics.

12. Fairy tale picture music

I learned this form of play with Vilmante Aleksiene.

- Purpose: Figures for identification are provided with a fitting fairy tale. With a period for individual drawing, associations can be reinforced and possibly connected with certain life episodes. During the musical expression that follows, emotions are intensified and made public. Topics dealing with life are stimulated.

- Procedure: The fairy tale is read aloud. Then the participants each draw a picture to the story. When done, they are asked to place the drawing on the floor, take an instrument and stand or sit next to the picture and express their feelings musically.

- Evaluation: Collection of topics and perhaps a feedback round.

Here I would also like to mention silence; mutual silence can promote transcendental topics.

6.5 Overview of Valid Musical Means for Targeted Warm-up

The following table summarizes music therapy interventions with regard to the emergence levels of the warm-up and their possible functions and effects.

Emergence Level	Intervention	Functions and Effects
Transcendental warm-up	• Meditative dances • Rituals • Work with ostinato • Adapt fairy tales • Poems • Look at pictures and use parts to play	• The senses are addressed • Transpersonal topics • Meaning of life • Perspectives • Spirituality
Social warm-up	• The senses are addressed • Transpersonal topics • Meaning of life • Perspectives • Spirituality	• Activation of interpersonal conflicts • Relationship experiences and transferences are stimulated • Getting to know others • Integration of new members
Mental warm-up	• Listening together to recorded music or live music	• Affects and moods are stimulated • Episodes associated with the sounds are remembered
Somatic warm-up	• Exercises, breathing, voice, movement, mimicry, gestures to music, working alone or in pairs for massage to music	• Energy increases • Individual topics are stimulated • Inner conflicts • Ambivalence • Better self-awareness

Table 7. Interventions and their Functions and Effects Corresponding to the Different Emergence Levels of Warming Up.

7 Stage and Spectator Area

Typical for psychodrama is the division of the room into two sections. Depending on the type of work, this is also recommended for music therapy. One section is the auditorium, discussion area, reality; the other section is the stage. On the stage everything is allowed, except breaking instruments or harming oneself or others.

This room division has several advantages:
- The stage raises the action above daily life. Representations on stage are artificial (or art). The stage enhances importance and attention.
- It helps the actors to feel like someone else and try something new or different because it is "only" a play. It is a space of the imagination where there is no "must", and everything is allowed.
- Being on stage is especially important for children. There they feel better heard and seen.
- The transition space from the auditorium to the stage can be used as a word barrier as well as for separating music from talking. Talking only takes place in the auditorium (with some exceptions). Whoever wants to talk moves to the auditorium. This transition from stage to reality space can aid the return to real age after a play with strong regressive phases. In therapy with children, work on this transition may already be an important therapeutic step. On stage, the child is allowed to act younger and to be re-nurtured. The path from the stage back to the spectator area, and the following discussion back in the actual age of the actor, are important therapeutic steps for many individuals, who can practice strategies for coming out of the regression and for their feeling of helplessness, and apply them when they suddenly feel small and helpless in real life.
- After a disturbing play, the conscious transition back to the real age and daily situations is also important for attaining a necessary 'roadworthiness.'
- The separation of auditorium and stage helps rationalizing individuals to remain in the play. By having to move to a different space, they are better able to realize their own continual avoidance behavior, and usually can soon improve their involvement in the play.
- The auditorium offers security and the possibility of self-regulation/control. One may return to it when one clearly wants to leave the play, escaping to it when the play becomes too much. Sometimes the therapist asks a player who is getting too overwhelmed to come to the spectator area. One may also simply sit in the auditorium and observe the stage; this applies mainly to group therapy.
- Listening is an important activity. Moreno was convinced of the therapeutic effect on spectators. Today we know that observing actions and empathizing affects us through mirror neurons (Bauer 2006). The spectator identifies with the action; his own experiences are recalled. For the actors on stage, being seen and

heard is important, and feedback from the spectators yields valuable suggestions and impulses for the process. The listener is invited to share and may give
feedback. "Only" listening is not "only" listening!

–   The place where the therapist sits or stands also has an important effect on the
    development of the play. If there is a possibility of re-traumatization or over-
    taxing of the protagonist, the therapist should stand near the stage. This usu-
    ally helps the protagonist find new solutions. However, if the goal is for the
    protagonist to get in touch with himself, and he expresses his situation, or if a
    group organizes itself musically, it is better for the therapist to remain in the
    auditorium.

For child and adolescent psychiatry, and in encounter groups as well as individual
and family sessions, this space division has proven useful.

Example from children's music therapy practice: transition between different spaces

Eleven-year old twins come to a session (the 6th). Both boys act aggressively in school towards teachers, Fred physically and Edi mainly verbally. They attend school separately, in
different classrooms. Edi talks about the anger that came over him during the week. He says
it is only because the two brothers are not allowed to be in school together. Separated, he
does not feel well. Edi does not want to play a scene from the past week, but he would like
to finally do something with his brother again. His brother Fred agrees that this is a good
idea and together they start building a cocoon on stage using gym hoops, a mattress and a
blanket, and they crawl into it.

I cannot see the inside of the cocoon. I begin to sing and to rock the cocoon. Inside it is very
quiet. I sing "Bajushki" (Russian lullaby) while continuing to rock them. I repeat the verses
and invent new ones and hum. After 20 minutes, I sit down next to the cocoon and wait. I
hear a soft sound of sucking. Slowly I push the blanket back and see two relaxed, contently
thumb-sucking boys, closely intertwined, a prenatal scene full of fragility. Tears come to my
eyes. Very slowly the two crawl out of their cocoon and sit down on the auditorium chairs.
The session is almost over.

We look at the cocoon and again they say that it was wonderful, and that they want to do
it again. My feedback: "I was very moved to see you all snuggled up next to each other, but
now you are strong young men again." I notice how both of them sit up a bit straighter,
which I interpret as a return to their actual age.

Back in their actual age, we go to the stage and clean up. Then we say goodbye in the auditorium.

In the following sessions the boys are able to enact their infantile powerlessness, which
they slip back into when they are treated unfairly by a person with authority. They rebuild
the cocoon without a cover, claiming that it is too warm inside. Edi insists that I help them
return emotionally from "Level 3" (our label for the regressive state) to "Level 11", their actual age. We develop a ritual: in the therapy session they sit on an auditorium chair and feel

in the "here and now". From this aspect they recall, if necessary, the "crash" scenes. With the help of this ritual the two become aware of their regressions in a constructive way; they also practice this outside of therapy and learn to catch and forgive themselves faster during regressions and outbreaks in school situations.

Sitting on an auditorium chair after one's own play means pausing to integrate perceptions, reflect, develop new behavior initiatives, and to come back to reality. After that, with an awareness of the therapy issues –perhaps after drawing or writing them down – one can again focus on daily duties and go back to work or head home confidently. Thus the auditorium has an important therapeutic function.

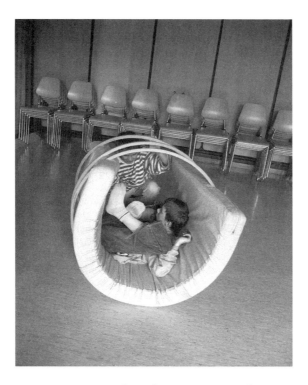

Figure 8. Cocoon without the Cover, Restaged

8 Scene Setting in Music Therapy

Scene setting on stage is done with instruments. In music therapy this means that instruments are selected for specific roles, set up and assigned. This phase can be very important and may take more time than the actual playing; sometimes it is not even necessary to play the instruments. Setting the scene, or staging, is an important process and arranging the instruments on stage often results in a discussion of the situation. Systemic psychology has adapted scene setting and calls it "installation". In psychodrama, scene setting is more versatile and is addressed with great care. Psychodramatic structures differ from most installation works and also from Tonius Timmermann's (2003) *"Klingende Systeme"* (Sounding Systems) mainly on two points:

1. The actors are carefully introduced to their roles (not just placed on stage). In this way the supporting actors, who might be affected by the topic, are prevented from acting out their own feelings and interfering with the protagonist's play.
   Introducing the role can already clarify it; taking on a role trains the supporting actors to empathize with the protagonist.
2. A clear distinction is made between scene setting (the installation) and the play. After the play, the scene is modified or a new scene is staged. This results in better recall and more lasting effects.

The following steps for scene setting have proven useful: We start with the discussion of the topic and formulate a "contract", which contains the precise issue that will be examined. The contract also contains the rule that the protagonist and the therapist may call for a stop at any time. Then the therapist together with the protagonist defines which situation, time frame and roles will be played. The therapist acts as director and when necessary, makes suggestions for the presentation. The protagonist is the author and is not responsible for how his subject is presented, but has the right to decide, with the therapist providing support.

When the play's approach has been settled, the therapist asks the protagonist to select an instrument for himself (or the main role) and to test the sound. In group therapy the protagonist chooses an auxiliary player (a double) for himself and introduces the chosen person. This allows him to change roles or to observe the role from a distance. In individual therapy the therapist can take on the auxiliary role.

For the remaining roles the protagonist chooses an instrument (or two) for each player, places it on the stage and plays in order show how it should sound for the planned role. In group therapy each choice of instrument is followed by the selection of a group member for each role and the introduction of the member to this role. The protagonist may ask, for example, "Are you playing my anxiety? It sounds fast and soft. As soon as the drum which represents my anger is played, the anxiety stops." Or, "You are playing my brother. He is 32 years old; he always looks after my mother and always plays when she plays". Choosing the roles, assigning the instruments and instructing the players how to play them already stimulates clarification of the roles for the protagonist.

Once the scene is assembled, the therapist and protagonist move to get some distance. Usually this is done by moving to the spectator area. The therapist lets the protagonist judge whether the stage is complete and appropriately arranged. Changes and additions can be carried out at this time.

During stage setting the therapist has the opportunity, or rather the duty, to prompt the patient to put an instrument or symbol on the stage which represents obvious, yet repressed or dissociated, aspects. If need be, the therapist can do this herself in discussion with the protagonist. Dissociated aspects are most often associated with fears, shame or other unpleasant feelings. If, as therapist, I choose a symbol for a dissociated feeling or attribute of the patient, I show him that I accept all his parts, including the ones he does not like—and I let him know that all the parts are valuable. In the Example from Practice in Chapter 4.2, I propose using the conga to represent the patient's uncontrolled anger. Because Claudio does not want the symbol for his anger on the stage, I suggest covering it with a cloth. Had he not agreed to this, I would have taken it from the stage and set it aside. It is important to gently and sympathetically make the patient aware of his dissociated part and to help him recognize it. Here, a discussion about it is already a helpful step.

The therapist is also responsible for noting any roles that may require a role reversal and to introduce them during the scene planning. The following is a summary:

Steps for scene setting

1. Clarify the exact topic
2. Clarify which scene will be played, indicating place and time represented
3. Clarify which roles will be played
4. Describe how are we staging, developing the scene
5. Install the "self" with an instrument (and auxiliary) on the stage
6. Choose the roles, instruments (and supporting actors)
7. Distance, overview and additions

Example from a family therapy practice: insight from scene setting and scene change

The Moser family is referred to music therapy by the school psychology service. Michael (10 years old) is rather small for his age, does not want to learn and is a terror at home. He torments his younger brother Paul (8 years old) and disobeys his mother. She feels totally overwhelmed. At school, Michael often tells made-up accident stories and heroic adventures, and he is often beaten and excluded by his classmates.

The father works shifts and often has to sleep during the day. Their home life is adjusted around his sleep schedule. When the children are noisy, watch out! Michael provokes and the mother gets blamed by the father when Michael disturbs his sleep. The younger brother Paul is well adjusted, quiet, obeys the mother, likes to read and is a good student.

In the consultation with the parents they agree to enter family therapy.

First family session:

Father, mother, son Michael and son Paul arrive. They come to therapy because of Michael, so he is the main person today. I declare, "You may choose an instrument for each family member, set them on the rug the way you want, and play for us the way you think your parents and your brother sound." (In my practice, the rug symbolizes the stage.) "They will then play the way you show them. After your playing we'll discuss it and decide together how to continue. The other family members may, if they like, do the same afterwards or in the next session."

He is visibly excited about choosing an instrument for each family member and about being able to set up the family the way he wants to. For his father he chooses the large accordion and plays it loudly. For himself he chooses the smaller accordion and he plays it more softly. He places both on center stage facing each other. For the younger brother he chooses a tambourine and taps it regularly. He puts it in the left back corner. He has to look towards the mother. For his mother he chooses a bird whistle and tweets loudly on it. He places her on the front left corner, facing the center. Now I ask the family to go on stage and pick up the instruments where Michal placed them, and to play the way Michael indicated. The mother is indignant; she does not want the small whistle. I suggest that for now she keep the instrument that Michael chose for her, and to tell us after the play how she felt about the whistle in the family orchestra. She agrees.

The play: Father and son play as loud as they can on the accordions. It sounds like a fight, but it is exciting and strong. Paul plays by himself, at a slow and regular beat on the tambourine. The mother tries desperately to make contact with the others on her small bird whistle. She has no chance, nobody listens; the accordions are so loud that sometimes the bird whistle cannot be heard at all. From time to time Paul acknowledges her by glancing towards her.

Feedback round: Father and Michael have enjoyed playing and fighting together. Both are content. Paul has no desire to participate in this loud noise making. He says that he is used to playing by himself. He liked his duo with his mother, but he had trouble hearing it next to the loud accordions. The mother says that this is exactly the way it is in the family: The father fighting and making noise with Michael, Paul withdrawing and her being lost in between. She cries. She says that sometimes she gets fed up with it and thinks about leaving. She agrees not to leave until the next session. The session ends.

Process: Having the family set-up carried out by the "problem" child is initially rejected by the mother. As they all get involved in playing, the music has its effect and all find Michael's representation adequate. The mother's suffering is triggered and manifested.

Second family session, 2 weeks later:

This time the mother speaks first and complains that Michael does not listen to her, and that she feels worthless and unwanted. The father is very moved. I suggest that the parents play together while I watch them with the sons.

Play: Father and mother choose djembes and drum together. The mother initially smiles, and then begins to cry. The father takes her into his arms. The sons watch, almost transfixed.

Conversation: The parents have not undertaken anything together in a long time. The mother starts mentioning her needs. The parents had wanted to plan a weekend alone for a long time, but were afraid that Michael would refuse to go to the grandparents, or would go on strike, or create somehow terror. Michael always wants to be included.

Scene change: "Father and Michael on Friday evening" – the scene is played verbally: The father tells Michael that he will be going away with mother and that Michael will be taken to his grandmother, as agreed. Michael says, "Out of the question!" The father answers, "I am not asking you, it will happen. Your mother and I need this time together." Michael shrugs his shoulders and says, "Well then!"

Feedback from the mother who has watched, "Now I feel much better and I'm looking forward to next weekend."

Scene change: Topic "Sunday evening, together again": Each family member picks an instrument; the parents take the djembes, Michael the accordion and Paul the recorder (which he is learning to play at a music school).

Rules of the game: When one person plays, everyone listens. When he or she is done, they imitate with their instruments what they have heard and remember, thereby showing that have listened attentively. The improvisation is played with pleasure and concentration. Each has something to say and wants to be heard.

Process: A different aspect is projected with each scene change. 1st scene: togetherness of the parents; 2nd scene: solidarity of the father with the mother and clear boundaries with Michael; 3rd scene: family discussion with appreciation and room for all.

Further sessions follow at 2-week intervals with more musical scenes: "In the morning when father sleeps", "The duo Michael and Paul", "The new family orchestra", "Father accompanies mother", "Mother accompanies father", "Everyone may play a solo."

The new solidarity between the parents and the carrying of responsibility by the father towards Michael brings peace and security to the family. Michael takes more responsibility for his behavior, and a change in his behavior becomes possible. The mother begins to assert her place in the family with the three men. Michael does his school work which improves his self-esteem and his status among his classmates. He is also beginning to play with his brother Paul and to help his mother (not without pleasure) with the cooking. Paul and his father have become closer. After half a year, family life is harmonious.

A musical play is often better than verbally played scenes. Music touches feelings directly and liberates energy for change. Musical psychodramatic plays are often more effective than counseling sessions, especially when children and adults are involved.

Arranging improvisations into named musical phrases that correspond to scenes from everyday life facilitates the transfer from therapy to life.

9 Scene Change in Music Therapy

Scene change in music therapy corresponds to a new movement in a piece of music. As a therapeutic intervention it offers many possibilities. It allows playing different aspects of a problem in sequence to develop time perspectives – be it "next time" or "in ten years", the meaning of life can be created. Behavior patterns can be played in parallel situations and may be changed and practiced, e. g., "How do I participate when somebody is already playing?" Repressed memories can resurface through repetition or variation of the subjects in different scenes. Transferences can be shown in parallel situations, as in the following example from practice with 17-year-old Max. Projections can be recognized and changes approached.

Example from therapy practice with a 17-year-old adolescent:
Recognition of behavior patterns and projections through scene changes

Max is 17 years old, has already quit his apprenticeship twice, refuses to go back to work and has become depressive. He is referred to therapy from career counseling.

In the first session he agrees to play musical improvisations with drums. In the second session I encourage him to represent his situation with his apprenticeship on the stage. For himself he chooses a small drum and for his boss the percussion set. Max plays himself on the drum, softly with a regular beat, controlled, almost inhibited. In portraying his boss on the percussion he works off steam. After that, the playing on his drum crumbles. Max describes how he cannot stand his boss and therefore is not returning to work. In the morning he cannot get up. I ask him to remember the first apprenticeship and to set it up and play on stage. He does not rearrange anything, but takes the same instruments and repeats the scene. I ask him if he knows other people or situations which would sound the same as that with him and his boss. He thinks for a moment and says, "Yes, with my father it is the same." In our conversation Max says that he can never do anything right for his father. He does not want to play this scene. In this session Max becomes aware of his fear of never being good enough. Through my feedback he realizes that he is very angry and that he can be very loud and energetic on the percussion. This resource becomes the therapy topic for the next session and helps Max express his strength and accumulated rage. His self-esteem is boosted. In looking back Max becomes aware of the regression he slips into as soon as a man shows superiority and power over him. He is now better able to relax and to mobilize his resources. The relationship with his father becomes the topic. Max is less and less affected by superior and important attitudes and learns to accept criticism through feedback, without feeling inferior.

In conversations with his parents and his second apprenticeship master, Max mentions his therapy experience, the play with the parallel experience (father/teacher), and how he wants to deal with his apprenticeship differently. They all understand that Max wants more positive responses for now, and that he may act somewhat less well-adapted and restrained. The boss shows understanding and benevolence, while the father is rather uncertain.

Process: The fear of not being good enough was probably the cause for Max's becoming insecure, slow, tense and progressively clumsy in his apprenticeship work. When the boss was impatient, Max felt like a small, helpless boy facing his father, and behaved like a child. Neither he nor the instructors knew how to deal with these regressions. Max became able to transform the bottled anger into life energy, and the depressive moods disappeared. The psychodramatic metaphor was comprehensible to all, and made the transfer from the therapy experience to daily life easier for all the participants – all without mentioning intimate family issues or moralizing. Max was able to continue his professional training.

The scene change helped uncover repressions and projections. Repressions, in contrast to dissociations, have constant, unconscious effects. They are repeated in different scenes and are often projected onto others. During musical improvisation they become audible, and with repetition they are seen as playful and morale-free, which facilitates integration. This also occurs in the next case where repressed issues come to light through frequent scene changes, and where roles can be modified.

Example from couples therapy practice: "Who sets the agenda?" Scene change uncovers dysfunctional behavior patterns

A quarreling couple comes to music therapy. The woman complains that the husband always "calls the shots" and that she always has to "dance to his tune". She says that she is fed up. He disagrees. He claims that she pushed him into couple's therapy.

Right in the first session I suggest that they each choose an instrument and play their "daily life situation" for me. He chooses the table drum, she chooses castanets and dancing. They change the scene several times after brief periods of play: "Early in the morning", "Sunday outing with the children", "going out together", "shopping tour". The wife makes the topic suggestions. The husband regularly waits a short time and then starts to play. The wife waits until he plays and then joins in hesitantly. He tries to adjust as fast as possible to her playing.

In the following conversation it is obvious that she is not used to starting and taking responsibility. At the same time she blames him for deciding on everything. She is not aware of his trying to adjust to her playing. He has taken responsibility for putting her impulses into play at the beginning and for harmonizing during the playing.

She shows impulses and wishes, but for the execution she relies on her partner. She views this dependence as an unpleasant dominance. She is unaware of her insecurity. He finds that he has always adjusted and done everything for his wife and family. He says that he does not understand what more she wants.

As the subsequent sessions showed, her behavior has a history: she would always have liked to determine more, but as the youngest child in the family, was only able to carry out her impulses when older siblings took them up.

The couple worked for a few more sessions by musically playing the sharing of responsibilities, the sensing of impulses, harmonizing, giving time to the partner, tolerating dissonance, and carrying through their own rhythms and melodies. During the verbal feedback rounds, self-confidence and self-esteem were strengthened.

Another way to use scene change is to change the surroundings. A problematic situation which is portrayed by a current experience in a team can be played in a subsequent scene in a marriage or in the family of origin. A dysfunctional behavior at school can be examined in parallel situations at home, at the sports club, etc., for its genesis, strengths and fixation, through enthusiastic play. Joy, and sometimes pain, which can emerge during the play, promote the motivation to change, and show where change can be applied. One can also play wish scenes which stimulate change, as shown in the following example.

Example from practice with a group in professional training:
"I don't want to be part of it, or do I?" Scene change from pain scenes to wish scenes allows the first step towards changing dysfunctional behavior patterns

Raul is 43, tall, athletic, strong, a professional therapist in special education. In his training group he has been an outsider for more than two years. For his topic, a group improvisation is chosen for the warm-up – a social warm-up in which he (again) participates as spectator. The situation is upsetting him, and he is not sure whether or not he wants to participate. He gives the impression of being a somewhat snooty outsider. He is ready to name the topic. He calls it, "It hurts whether I belong or not." He says that he has known this pain since starting school, when he had physical problems and was weaker than his classmates.

The first scene represents his home before the first day of school. For his mother he chooses a lyre and for himself a guitar, for his father who sits far away and faces away, he chooses the Irish drum, but does not allow him to play it. He and his mother play together. She faces him tenderly. The father is 'absent', soundless, sitting facing away from the family.

The second scene is at school. The teacher (tambourine) sits across from two students (with rattles). They are school friends of Raul. He sits next to them with the guitar. The teacher beats furiously on the tambourine and the two friends with the rattles play happily with him. Raul (guitar) tries briefly to get into musical contact with the classmates. He is afraid of the teacher and he stops playing. He no longer wants to participate, – or does he? Tears well up with great intensity.

The scene is repeated with Raul's auxiliary player, so he can hear from the auditorium how this group of men (teacher and classmates) sounds, and how lost he is with the guitar trying to make contact. Raul's tears continue to flow.

During the role feedback Raul's double (auxiliary player) says that during the play he wanted to scream, "Father, I need you! Father, help me!" I suggest a scene with Raul and his father. In the scene, "Raul and his father" it is clear that there is no chance for Raul to get support from his father. The father is entirely focused on his job and avoids the children and their problems.

The question is, what would Raul have needed or wished for himself? Raul does not know. Now the identification of the role carriers becomes important. The next scene is arranged by Raul's double and the actor playing the father. They suggest, "Raul has a father who listens to him." The father now plays on the Irish drum, accompanying his guitar-playing son. Then the father gives the teacher a piece of his mind (musically). The teacher has no other choice than to join in with the tambourine.

After this scene, Raul is again agitated and confirms that he would have liked it to be like that. He is not ready to play the scenes with the supportive father; it would be too painful. The group is very moved and urges Raul to be taken into their midst. He agrees to be rocked in a wool blanket. The group sings Bajushki. Raul relaxes and feels secure in the group.

In the final round Raul says, "The play with the energetic father who gives his strong piece of mind to the teacher made me aware that I often defend weak children in such situations, and am very good at it". Raul feels that he has the requirements to stand up for himself in groups and wants to practice this.

Process: The clearly named change of scene touches on Raul's ambivalent mix of feelings: the security with his mother, the absence of a father, exposure in groups, and a wish for security outside of the mother-son relationship. The wish scenes are first developed by the actors, allowing Raul to become aware of his repressed needs. During these he also becomes aware of his resources. In the final scene, the rocking scene with Raul being carried by the group, he has the positive experience of "belonging".

Targeted, titled scene changes help uncover dysfunctional behavior patterns. Representation with music deepens the emotional experience, frees energy for change in the protagonist and the group, and can open access to resources.

Play forms for scene changes in music therapy correspond to new musical movements

1. "From all sides"

- Purpose: A problem is presented from different perspectives or by different individuals in order to find new insight and approaches to solutions.

- Procedure: If different opinions are known, they can be set up from the beginning and then played like a suite. New movements can be composed throughout.

- Evaluation: Sharing/feedback round

2. Perspectives

- Purpose: To develop perspectives; to change "next time" in the desired direction; to develop goals and meaning in life.

- Procedure: Appropriate scenes are developed in sequence, e. g., "today and in 10 years" or "reality-scene and wish-scene".

- Evaluation: If possible, the next step in the desired direction is defined.

3. Rondo: "The next step"

"The longest path starts with the first step". This saying is the foundation for this exercise. In difficult life situations courage for the next step is often lost, or the direction or correct order of steps is not clear. A slow recovery is often only possible when the "next step" or the "first step in a different direction" forms a topic. The following play is useful for the end of a long group session or therapy phase.

- Purpose: Insight becomes expanded by group members and transfer to everyday life can be boosted and supported by the group. With the play "the next step", possibilities for transfer are weighed, and fears and resistance can be overcome. The "rondo" format enhances the play's sustainability.

- Procedure: At the end of a group session each member presents his next step in a short play on stage. This next step scene should show an action for a determined time. Between the scenes, the same short motif is played each time in order to form a rondo which connects the individual scenes and allows the next player enough time to get ready on stage. The motif may be a gong sound, the sound of a 'singing' bowl, an ostinato, or a simple melody that is easy to remember. The motif provides a frame and makes the memory of the experience easier to recall. It provides a framework and a foothold.

- Evaluation: It is possible for the members to support each other and to establish "contracts". If someone needs reinforcement, they can, for example, agree to a phone call when the next step is planned.

4. "Where else does this occur?"

- Purpose: To create awareness of transferences and behavior patterns, to bring repressions to the foreground through repetition and variation of the topic; to aid recognition of problematic projections, and approach changes.

- Procedure: After playing a scene one asks for similar scenes and plays them, too (see "Example from Practice with a 17-year-old adolescent").

- Evaluation: Behavior patterns emerge.

5. "Theme and Variations"

- Purpose: To change or practice behavior patterns in parallel situations; to be inspired by the creativity and experience of group members. To learn other customs or morals; to expand social competence.

- Procedure: A topic is chosen. A corresponding scene is set up. The participants play variations on the same topic, separately or in groups, one after the other, e. g., "How do I tell my boss?" "How do I join in when there are two already playing together?" "How do I get attention?" etc.

- Evaluation: Spectator feedback.

10 Role Clusters in Music Therapy

Music therapy is particularly well suited for work on role clusters, since the concurrency of different roles can resound musically. The blending of our roles can be represented musically and unraveled and changed with the help of psychodramatic elements.

For instance, the role "child" is an extensive role cluster consisting of neighbor, student, classmate, friend, perhaps animal caretaker (for the family pet), perhaps violin player, teammate in soccer, perhaps patient. Somatic roles, such as eater and sleeper, are also part of this role cluster. Psychological roles are also important: crying, screaming, laughing, fearful, and content roles. All together, these form a complex role cluster. When the roles are working well together, we are hardly aware of them. When certain role components are dysfunctional, however, problems may arise which disturb the role cluster or cause mental and somatic illness. Here are some examples from therapies with children: A traumatic family experience can affect school performance; a problem at school can result in "acting out" at home, or cause somatic reactions such as loss of appetite, sleep disturbances, etc. In psychodrama we now have the possibility of unraveling these role clusters and examining the roles separately. On stage, different role aspects can be presented in an exciting way, and their functions made apparent. Well-functioning roles may be used as resources and dysfunctional roles can be changed or dismissed. For example, if a child performs poorly in school, the problem could be rooted in very different role aspects. As the "mother's child" or as "father's child", e. g., one of the parents may be demanding too much or be overwhelming for non-obvious reasons (illness, depression, alcoholism) and the child may be enmeshed in solidarity conflicts. It may also be that a child feels inadequate compared to a more gifted sibling and in competing, overtaxes himself (sibling role). By playing the individual roles, these problems can come to light.

Of course, the cause of the problem may be in the student role itself. The student role, which is in itself a role cluster, may be further dissected into relationship roles, such as Student of Teacher A, Student of teacher B, Classmate of C, Desk mate of D, etc. A troubled relationship with a teacher or classmate may be a reason for failure, fear and/or refusal to attend school. Cognitive overtaxing can cause similar symptoms.

To work on this cluster we can organize the roles according to school subjects: student in language, math, physical education, etc. A one-sided weakness or giftedness can cause different problems. One may also divide by activities. Roles such as writer, reader, homework-completer, participant in classroom discussions, math problem solver, artist, etc., can give clues to problems. With these activities one addresses mainly the physical roles. These may reveal physical impairments requiring further clarification, such as vision or hearing problems, weakness in multi-tasking or inability to think abstractly, etc. Problems in work behavior or work situations can also have different causes that may be incomprehensible initially. Play with roles uncovers which role components work well and can be used as resources, and which ones need changing. With the addition of targeted educational support (not just therapy), it is usually possible to change dysfunctional role behavior and remodel various parts of the role cluster. This is so even if it involves accepting or tolerating weaknesses and mental overload, rather than feeling ashamed or drowning in negative feelings. Even the discovery of physical limitations for which there are no direct remedies can be a relief for the concerned. They can understand themselves better and others may offer them more understanding.

Example from music therapy practice with an 11-year-old girl: work with role clusters for the analysis of school problems

Melanie, an 11-year-old girl with an immigrant background moved here from a different Swiss city half a year ago and entered 4th grade. She is referred to music therapy because she often refuses to cooperate at school, has little endurance, works superficially, acts withdrawn in class and is rude during recess. She also began missing school now and then.

She likes coming to music therapy. She enjoys playing music with me and gains confidence. In the third session she agrees to work on the role cluster "student". She chooses the following roles and instruments:

1. "Classmate", djembe
2. "Student in Mr. B's class", small maracas
3. "Student doing homework", glockenspiel
4. "Writing student" (the worst part of school, she says), a rattle

She plays one instrument after the other. As "classmate" with the djembe she plays lively, rhythmically and loud. The title of the piece is, "Playing with girl friends". She asserts that she has friends even though she joined in the middle of the school year. As "student in Mr. B's class" she turns the maracas very slowly; a soft drizzle is audible. Title: "Fear of making mistakes". As "student doing homework" she plays a few notes on the xylophone and then casually sweeps the mallet over the wooden bars. Title: "I don't feel like it!" As "writing student" she moves the rattle only a little, then more and more intensively, culminating in a "furioso". Title: "Writing is shit!" Upon my feedback she tells me that the teachers have always criticized her writing, ever since she started school. Again today, Mr. B tore up a page of her writing and two boys laughed. She complains about the teacher in strong language. She says that he does not like her. I ask her if she would agree to talk to the teacher with me. She agrees and is ready to participate.

We set up a meeting. Mr. B is very cooperative. He shows us her notebooks and worksheets and explains that Melanie sometimes does not write on the lines and sometimes writes anywhere on the page. She yells out that she cannot do it any better and that she tried her best, and starts to cry. The suspicion arises that she may not see clearly. The teacher had already asked the school physician and was told that the eye exam at the beginning of school was normal. She thinks that her vision is good and that she does not need glasses. A further point I am addressing is mocking by other students. Mr. B explains to Melanie that she makes faces at the class when he asks her to do something and that it makes the classmates laugh. He says that he finds her behavior very annoying. We agree that Mr. B will be tolerant with Melanie's writing if she agrees to see an eye doctor. Mr. B will reprimand the students who laugh at her, as long as she is ready to control her grimacing. Melanie agrees. I contact the parents regarding an eye appointment.

Distinguishing the different roles of Melanie's "student "role cluster leads to constructive changes. In the discussions with the teacher she feels active in shaping her student role. Melanie's relationship with Mr. B and other teachers improves and she attends school regularly.

The exam at the eye clinic shows a problem with the eye muscles which is surgically correctable in adults. She gets glasses which she often "forgets" at home. For music therapy many topics remain, such as "fear of making mistakes", along with the question of "Who am I?" These topics can be more easily worked on now that Melanie is ready to be more aware of her mental and physical strengths and weaknesses. In particular, her resources, her empathy, and the ability to form friendships become a positive awareness and motivate her to go to school and help her solve school problems and accept shortcomings.

A person who felt like a failure before therapy can, by working on role clusters, regain awareness of well-functioning roles. Confidence and the ability to act are strengthened, and roles that need changing can be adjusted through access to the individual's own resources. Weaknesses can be integrated with the best possible outcome.

Work with role clusters can provide identity and be very helpful for people with immigrant backgrounds or identity problems. Awareness of the multitude of roles helps recognize and reinforce one's own essence. With growing self-confidence, fear of the unknown disappears, and forces to change the dysfunctional roles become available.

Work on role clusters is also valuable as an intervention in supervision. The role spheres which show symptoms are often not the same as the ones manifesting problems. By analyzing these shifts, new approaches to treatment can open up.

Play modes for role clusters

Psychodrama offers various interventions for musical play with role clusters.

1. Setting up the inner orchestra

• Purpose: Awareness of role components, strengthening of resources and changing of dysfunctional patterns.

• Procedure: The protagonist explores his situation in conversation with the therapist who, with questions, helps to identify roles. She then picks an instrument, plays it and looks for a supporting actor. The protagonist introduces the actor to his role and gives instructions on how to play it (this is different from the installation work described by Timmermann 2003). The cluster is played, all parts simultaneously or in sequence. The protagonist can act like a conductor and change the sound or position of certain roles, and can ask for a new movement to be played. Scene changes are also possible where a role is further subdivided (see "Example from music therapy practice with an 11-year-old girl" at the beginning of this chapter). The protagonist may also play partial roles in a duet with other roles. In group therapy, the protagonist has the possibility of trying out each position in the orchestra.

- Evaluation: Feedback regarding the role components with well-functioning resources empowers the protagonist.

2. „Babuschka"

- Purpose: A fixed behavior that is causing problems is seen as a layered behavior. The habits that cause the problems today have a history. Often they made sense in the past and were real resources, but now they need to be changed. With the "Babushka" play, hidden causes can come to light. They may be resources, painful episodes, acquired values, all components that can be used for change. Self-acceptance is promoted.

- Procedure: Scene setting begins in the present; deciding how the topic sounds for scene setting today, choosing instruments and actors. Then the presentation shows how it was, e. g., 5 years ago, 10 years ago, back to the first memories.

- Evaluation: From the overview of the past developments, resources and prominent injuries, the current process is further developed.

3. "In the same boat"

This form of play is good for groups whose members are confronted with similar problem situations, such as mothers, training groups, patient groups, and self help groups.

- Purpose: To enhance self-image as well as the identity perceived by others. Professional identity and possibly a new orientation can be stimulated. Strategies for solutions can be expanded.

- Procedure: Each group member draws her role cluster relating to the problem being addressed. The drawings are examined by the group and the therapist asks questions and gives advice regarding role layers. Then the group decides what will be played. This can be a substitute role cluster for the group or a scene created together.

Advice for scene development: It is best to first arrange pleasant, well-functioning roles with the instruments in order to find energy for the difficult components. Different role components that are seen in several drawings can be arranged as an orchestra.

The scene setting corresponds to an orchestra structure. There may be registers with several members playing the same cluster component.

Now the play and its variations can begin.

• Evaluation: Sharing and feedback round. New aspects are named and ideas for solutions exchanged.

11 Role Reversal/Role Exchange and Doubling/Mirroring in Music Therapy

Role reversal, role exchange, doubling and mirroring are further interventions which may also be applied in music therapy in order to expand insight and processes.

11.1 Role Reversal

If a person can imagine himself as somebody else, role reversal can be an effective intervention, especially when followed by a sharing/feedback round.

Role reversal in therapy is always done between relationship partners to promote empathy. When one plays in a duet with the partner's instrument in the manner that he or she plays it, one can feel like the partner. The role reversal aids "you-awareness" and relationship understanding.

- Seeing oneself played by another person in a role reversal, and receiving feedback from the other person, one's identity can be broadened. Feedback after a role reversal with a relationship partner can help integrate dissociated parts and lead to discovery of new parts of oneself.
- By having the opportunity to play a polar opposite in a role reversal, these inner opposites may also be found within ourselves. The recognition that, "I can play this too!" supports the remodeling of old relationship patterns. Role reversal encourages empathy by allowing one to act like the partner. The inability to perform role reversals provides diagnostic clues (e. g., traumatization, cognitive impairment, autistic traits). In cases of suspected abuse, extreme caution is advised. If a traumatized person plays the aggressor he may (again) identify with the aggressor and "lose" himself. Aggression directed against the victim in a play can promote suicidal behavior.

Since role reversal is always about the exchange of positions between two partners, no additional plays will be suggested.

11.2 Role Exchange

Role exchange has entirely different functions and effects from role reversal. In music therapy it can be practiced by playing instruments.

- Role exchange promotes self-esteem
- allows recognition of acquired values
- makes repressions audible
- can bring out 'floating' aspects and diffuse fears so that they may be assigned.
- It allows one to try out new things and to expand role flexibility.

When role fixation becomes apparent in a therapy, it can be resolved with role exchange play.

Play modes with role exchange in music therapy

1. Improvisation with place exchange and instrument exchange

- Purpose: Exchange of designated instruments promotes flexibility on different levels. The musical function of a gong is different from that of a kalimba; the manner of playing it is different as well. The playful format of the exchange of instruments encourages playing instruments which one would not have chosen, enabling expansion of the self-image. New approaches are tested.

- Procedure: Instruments is set up around a circle and the participants sit down and improvise on them together. One person (possibly the therapist) directs the instrument exchange. The players pass their instrument on to the next person or change places.

2. Solo – Tutti

- Purpose: To accompany the group and, alternatively, be accompanied by the group as a soloist, encourages self-esteem and role flexibility.

- Procedure: A group (or two people) plays, alternating the solo and accompaniment. This is a well known play in music therapy with many variations.

3. Musical functions

- Purpose: To practice social flexibility. Fixations and repressions, as well as floating components, may become audible; for example, a person consistently exhibits an oddity, playing too softly or always faster than the others.

- Course of action: Distinction is made not only between soloists and the "tutti" group, but one group may be responsible for pace, one for rhythm, one for bass, one for harmony, and one for melody. These functions can be exchanged by exchanging the instruments. With practiced participants it is also possible to take on several functions with a given instrument (drum circle plays may be used too).

- Variation: Functions such as pace, rhythm, harmony, melody and direction are led by one individual and exchanged.

- Evaluation: Answering the questions: With which function am I most comfortable? What do I want to develop more? Feedback round.

4. The "opposite" or the "anti-role"

- Purpose: Group challenges! Participants are playfully confronted with repressions and dissociations, which facilitates analysis. This mode of play may be very confrontational, but also humorous and exciting.

- Procedure: The group is divided into two subgroups. Each subgroup determines opposite roles for the participants of the other group, which are then assigned. They may be symbolic, imaginary roles such as "hummingbird", "old turtle", "stag in heat", "water lily in the pond", or professional roles such as "secretary taking dictation", or "vacationer in a lounge chair". They may also be musical roles: "metronome for the group", "conductor", or "echo".

  Each participant has to implement his role in the next improvisation. The play may be composed as a suite, a rondo, or it may be improvised by the two groups and played one after the other.

- Evaluation: Detailed feedback.

5. Circle play

I learned this type of play with Katja Loos.

- Purpose: To make contact and quickly enter into an "existing relationship" and then say goodbye; promotes flexibility. Acquired values and habits can be recognized and changed. Feelings of loneliness and fear can surface.

- Procedure: The participants sit around a circle with an instrument. Person 1 starts playing. Next to him or her, Person 2 enters the play. As soon as Person 3 starts, Person 1 leaves the trio. Then Person 4 can enter and Person 2 leaves, etc. If, after one or several rounds, the direction is reversed, new challenges arise.

- Evaluation: Sharing round.

11.3 "Doubling" and "Mirroring"

Role exchange has entirely different functions and effects from role reversal. In music therapy it can be practiced by playing instruments. Role exchange promotes self-esteem, allows recognition of acquired values, makes repressions audible, and can bring out 'floating' aspects and diffuse fears so that they may be assigned. It allows one to try out new things and to expand role flexibility.
When role fixation becomes apparent in a therapy, it can be resolved with role exchange play.

The double can provide new suggestions and variations, thereby encouraging changes. The protagonist may listen from the auditorium or play along like a register in the orchestra in order to try and practice new things.

In mirroring, the double allows the protagonist to distance himself, seeing and hearing himself from a distance (from the auditorium) as the double repeats the protagonist's play as accurately as possible. This aids self knowledge and makes behavior patterns more obvious and changeable. The distance of the protagonist can help him relax and build energy for creative changes.
    Doubling and mirroring are interventions in protagonist plays. Mirroring may also be used in social warming up, synchronization, or in concentration/attention training, as well as in the development of "leadership qualities".

Play modes for mirroring in music therapy

1. The mirroring duet
• Purpose: Attention training and development of leadership qualities. The more predictable the leading person is, the easier it is to follow him. The better the leading person is at judging the response possibilities of the imitators, the more successful the synchronization.

• Procedure: Two people improvise together musically, or one person plays and the other moves to the music. The spectators have to decide who is leading and setting the impulses.

2. Two dancers in front of the mirror:
• Purpose: Practice movement coordination, mutual suggestion of new movement patterns.

• Procedure: One person plays an instrument. Two other people face each other, like in front of a mirror, and move.
    – Variation 1: One person leads, the other follows
    – Variation 2: Both are so in tune with each other that leading and following become unimportant; they can change rapidly, and each can inspire the other

3. In the "hall of mirrors"

• Purpose: Stimulates imagination; useful for somatic warming up.

• Procedure: One person moves to music (may be on CD) and the others in the room imitate her. Here too, the leading person may "take" the group along or let it go, depending on how predictably she moves and how aware she is of the participants' abilities.

4. "Echo"

• Purpose: Mirroring out of sync trains not only the ability to observe but also the ability to multi-task musically. Since music always involves movement and expression, sound automatically triggers movement mentally and stimulates a feeling. Repetition of the same musical phrase trains the recall of the movement pattern and the feeling. This exercise can stimulate attentiveness, empathy and short term memory.

• Procedure: One person plays a musical, easily repeatable, motif. The length of the motif must be determined depending on the participants, e. g., no longer than two times four notes/beats. Another person plays the echo and may then play the next motif.
  – Variation 1: The motif is repeated by the whole group and the degree of difficulty is increased.
  – Variation 2: The motif is played around a circle – one person after the other – with different instruments. The goal is to remember the original motif, despite possible variations, and to repeat it.

Mirror plays and plays from the chapter on role exchange also lend themselves well to allowing a group to get familiar with the instruments.

12 Sociometry in Music Therapy

Sociometry, a widely known and applied method developed by J. L. Moreno, comes from psychodrama. Using sociometry, highly effective but hidden networks in groups can become evident and brought to awareness. In music therapy it is possible to use non-musical methods such as the sociogram, which is a graphic representation of the relationships in a group. Sociograms are created from observing groups or talking with group members. Their answers can then be charted graphically, represented musically, or enacted in scenes on stage. Since graphic sociograms are widely used in therapy, I will not discuss them further but rather present "music therapeutic sociograms". In music therapy the following aims can be pursued with sociometry: promotion of familiarity in the group, exposure of group structures, integration of outsiders, solving of group problems, and gathering and fostering group energy.

12.1 Promoting a degree of familiarity in groups

A degree of familiarity between group members in a therapy group is the basis for trust. The level of acquaintanceship with the therapist is also important. We promote this sociometrically by discovering old acquaintanceships, as well as by building new ones.

Sociometric play modes to improve familiarity

Play modes are different from social warming up in that existing connections and relationships between individuals are uncovered.

1. Who knows whom?

- Purpose: To show who in the group knows whom and what type of relationships exist. It also becomes apparent who does not yet know anybody. This is often important for the well-being of a group; otherwise there is a danger of existing familiarity between certain members being misinterpreted.

- Preparation: Lay out small instruments that can be easily played while walking around.

- Procedure: Each person chooses an instrument and stands on the stage next to people he already knew before the session. In this way subgroups are formed which then in turn play together. People who belong to several groups play with each of these groups. The degree of familiarity becomes apparent; it also becomes obvious who does not yet know anybody. The latter can now play together. If there is only one person who is new in the group, he can now understand his situation better. For further integration, the next exercise may be useful.

2. Integration of "single" participants

- Purpose: "Single" individuals have the opportunity to find common ground with other group members in order to develop a sense of belonging.

- Preparation: As in the exercise "Who knows whom?"

- Action: First the therapist looks for common criteria since she knows a few things about the participants, e. g., profession, domicile, education. She builds improvisation groups according to these criteria.

  After a while, the participants may name other criteria based on interests, and new subgroups may be formed, e. g., "Who plays the piano? Come over here, please!" "Who has children?" "Who loves pizza?" Preferences, origins, jobs, etc., can be asked about in a playful way. The people who fit each of the characteristics get together and improvise. This way, a group with common interests can be created in a few minutes.

- Evaluation: A verbal sharing/feedback round can provide information about the changes in group structure and the mental state of the participants.

12.2 Revealing Group Structures

Through sociometry, the therapist and group members recognize the group structure. Revealing the group structure is not only helpful for new people to connect, but it helps all group or team members to find their place. When the structures are hidden, the members often think that the other members are more interesting or important. They do not understand why others talk more with each other, have more eye contact or drink coffee together during breaks, and they feel excluded. With sociometry, it is possible to have more clarity about the situation.

Example from practice of sociometric music therapeutic integration work
Excerpt from therapy with a child (School Psychology Service)

Kim, a second grader, became more and more withdrawn; he did not like to go to school and fell behind scholastically. He was therefore referred to music therapy.

Kim appears to be depressed. In individual music therapy he does not exhibit any abnormalities, but complains, without naming "enemies", that nobody wants to play with him or volunteers to work with him. In class he feels like an outsider. His parents and his teacher confirm this, but do not think that there is bullying involved, as I initially suspected. I suggest a sociometric inquiry, which the teacher performs. She questions her students on three topics; for each question, four classmates may be named. "Who are your favorite playmates during recess?" "Who do like to work with in class?" "Who do you play with after school?" Kim, the outsider, was never named in these choices. It turned out that the class consisted of four groups which chose each other for work, play and free time. A further analysis showed that each of these four groups consisted of children who had attended the same neighborhood kindergartens. They already knew each other a minimum of three years, some for eight as neighbors. Only now do we find out that Kim had moved here, to a new apartment complex, shortly before the beginning of the school year. He was the only student who did not know any of his schoolmates, and was therefore more shy, although initially eager to make contact. Neither he nor his parents nor the other children were aware of this situation. The teacher, who was new to the school, was also unaware of this background. We were all surprised by the intense long-term effect of the "kindergarten teams". The group members support each other almost like family members, and walk home from school together. The new student is not recognized as such; he is simply less popular and does not get much attention. He lives in the new buildings where none of the others live. After recognizing the situation, we discuss it with the class. Kim is very relieved.

Instead of individual therapy, class sessions (90 minutes) are planned and carried out as a "music project" in a large auditorium. (Kim is not mentioned in this context). The music therapist and the teacher lead together, with the teacher taking on the educational tasks and the therapist leading the exercises and the feedback rounds. During the first exercise, the students can invite each other for musical interactions. Whoever has an idea, invites somebody else. This teaches them to play the instruments and to improvise. In the following play there is a hoop on the floor; each student is allowed to step into the hoop and to try to making musical contact with the students outside the hoop who play their instruments. However, the person in the hoop is the "outsider" with whom nobody plays or interacts. In this role exchange, all of them feel for a brief time what it means not to have any response from a group, despite trying. After a feedback round we conclude in unison with a rhythmic improvisation.

At the beginning of the second session, every student can play with each other student as a social warm-up. Kim now has the opportunity to improvise with each classmate. In the feedback round, beautiful moments are recounted. We conclude again with a group improvisation.

In the following session, groups are formed according to their favorite instruments, native language and favorite foods. This opens up the kindergarten groups somewhat and Kim becomes less shy and dares to talk with other students, even outside the "music lessons".

After a few weeks, two additional sessions with music therapeutic integration work followed, and were very much enjoyed by all. An individual therapy, without group sociometry and group therapy, would most likely not have brought such a positive result in such a short time (10 times 45 min. for nine weeks).

Sociometric forms of play to reveal group structures

Sociometry is the method of choice to reveal group structures.

1. "Group history"

- Purpose: With a chronologic set-up of the group, its development becomes clear and changeable. Through musical expression, feelings and moods become audible. This exercise is useful for therapy groups, for team development, organizations and school classes. Because feelings in the group are expressed musically and not verbally, these "statements" are more spontaneous, hardly morally condemnable, and in general much more honest than verbal statements.

- Preparation: A spot in the room is designated as 'point zero'. From this point a line leads to a point representing the present. Instruments are placed at the present time point. A scale (from zero to the present) may be represented as years, months, etc.

- It may be that from a given organization no one among the group participants was present at point zero. An instrument can be set there, symbolically representing the founder or the founding of the organization.

- Procedure: The group members gather at the point representing the present. The participant who has been with the organization for the longest time, remembers the circumstances when he joined, and taking an instrument, stands near the corresponding point on the time scale, and plays how he feels. The next person also takes a spot on the scale and plays. Then the two participants play together, expressing how they felt at the time. This way the organization can be represented chronologically. At certain times several people may be joining. The therapist follows the musical development of the individual members.

- Evaluation: Sharing can take place verbally while still standing on the time scale. The therapist or group members can address noticeable changes, which may be discussed later. Subsequently, the scene may be ended. The ensuing feedback consists of observations by the therapist and the participants.

2. Elections: "Who wants to be with whom?"

- Purpose: Using elections, groups can be "x-rayed". The distribution of popularity in a group can be exposed. Is there a star one wants to be close to? Are there couples? Are there loners or outsiders? Does the group regulate itself and look for "justice"? Subgroups can also be assessed. Are elections one-sided or are they mutual?

- Preparation: Since not every participant likes to do the same thing with every one of the other participants, it is necessary to develop criteria which are appropriate for the group. For a school class it might be, "Enjoy playing together", "Enjoy playing on a team together", "Enjoy doing homework together". In a music therapy training group it could be "Improvising together", "Working on theoretical topics together", "Leading a group together", or "Opening a practice together". Instruments which can be carried around are set up.

- Procedure: Once the topic is chosen, each member takes an instrument and looks for the person(s) she would like to be with and "plays at" that person. This continues until everybody stands still. Then the therapist stops the music. The scenes are "frozen", i. e., all stand still and look at one another (perhaps photos are taken).

- Evaluation: Sharing/feedback round. The therapist, who is the only spectator, gives feedback about the process of selection. Members who were not chosen are now at the center. They could be victims of bullying or be part of "the wrong crowd" in the group. Perhaps they have to do their "homework" to stay in the group. Feedback "gifts" are helpful at this point and especially important for the "non-chosen".

Setting the group up musically is "softer" than a written sociogram because the choices may be influenced during the play and by the play. With written sociograms, each person decides alone and the results are subsequently evaluated. Either way, hidden yet important and effective networks are uncovered.

3. "Scale"

- Purpose: Show who has a lot of experience, knowledge or interests. This may be useful at the beginning of a seminar.

- Procedure: The participants choose a point on the scale or range where they judge themselves to be; e. g., people who have no experience in music therapy stand at the beginning of the line, people who are professionals with a lot of experience stand at the other end. The rest of the participants, candidates, students or graduates, choose different points. This allows an overview of the group composition within minutes.

12.3 Group Energy

In order to work carefully with groups, it is important for the therapist to have a good overview of the current issues and the energy level of the group, and to be able to make it visible. The number of people who support a certain topic or a protagonist indicates which subject or person attracts the most energy at that moment. If the group proposes several topics, or several protagonists are ready to bring up their issues, it may be very helpful for the group to choose the topic sociometrically. The topic chosen by the largest number of participants is staged. This may be difficult for group members who are eager to play, yet are not chosen. There are several reasons why a group or one of its members might not back a person or topic: The topic may be too 'hot' or too strange, the group may be too tired, another topic may in the air, or the group member not chosen may not be well integrated. All of these are reasons to look more carefully and possibly not to proceed, even if the therapist has trouble doing so. When such an energy-laden situation is overlooked or misjudged by the director or therapist (because he is glad that someone volunteers to play), the danger exists that a protagonist may "overheat". A re-traumatization or overtaxing of individual members or of the entire group is possible. It makes sense in such situations to ask the group first or to apply sociometric analyses to make sure there is enough support in the group for a topic or a person.

It is also possible that a protagonist refuses to play when she feels that the whole group is pressing too hard. This must be respected in order to prevent the group from acting out something at the expense of the protagonist. One side effect of sociometric selection is that group members learn to constructively use selections and rejections, common in daily life, and to accept, or at least evaluate them.

An offer of improvisation to the topic for the whole group, in which one is free to play on stage or to listen, can relax such situations.

Example from practice with a 56-year-old woman whose mother-issue is not chosen by the group

Jutta is 56 years old, director of a community college, and has been part of an encounter group with nine women for the last two years. During the last three sessions, mother-daughter problems have been brought to the stage. Being a mother, she often had to "bang the big drum" in these plays. Today, after the social warm-up, she mentions her topic wish for the second time, "Guilt feelings regarding the deceased mother". Dora also comes forward and would like to play the situation between her children and her mother. Verena moans that she is fed up with "mother plays". We choose sociometrically. Dora's topic has five votes, Jutta's none. Verena stands next to another member in the auditorium. The group makes sure that all members get a chance to participate. I ask Jutta if she could join in Dora's choice of play. She takes a deep breath and says energetically that in her opinion it should be her turn now. The participants look at me in suspense. I suggest a group improvisation to the theme: "Every daughter has a mother". They all agree.

My instructions are: "On the left is the mother corner and on the right the daughter corner. Every woman can go on stage with an instrument or stay in the auditorium. You are allowed to change instruments and/or move to different areas."

The nine women choose mainly drums, Verena chooses a flute. They scatter around the stage. Dora sits down in the middle. The improvisation starts with a quiet pulse from the mothers' corner. Verena starts to play a virtuoso melody on the flute. Then two groups form, facing each other, competing in volume and tempo; the participants change groups from time to time. Soon a lively, joyful improvisation develops. In the end the players all hug each other and laugh!

Comments during the sharing round: "It was fun to fight with the mother." "I gave the daughter a piece of my mind." – "I identify with the mother." Verena enjoyed the beginning pulse which supported her during her solo. Jutta said that on stage she suddenly felt like a mother. She said that, after all, she had also become a mother (caretaker) for her mother in the end, and had tried her best. But her mother was never satisfied. So during the improvisation she became the daughter again and let the ungrateful mother have it loud and clear with her banging on the drum. Dora says that she felt solidarity with the daughters who do not want the mothers to meddle. Eventually she let the topic drop and just enjoyed the play. Other women had the same experience. The tension which had been present at the beginning was gone.

Jutta also had her turn in the play. It started with reproach for the group for which she had often played "mother" on the drum. This fed her anger which loomed behind the feelings of guilt and self blame. (The group can be seen as the "ungrateful mother".) Aggression against the beloved, mourned and ungrateful mother got reinforced with the play, expressed and conscious.

Approaches for exposing group energy

1. Choice of topics on stage

- Purpose: To establish how many participants choose a certain topic and are ready to take it on.

- Procedure: Proposed topics are set up on stage and represented by a person or an instrument. Participants stand next to their preferred topic.

- Evaluation: When the set up is complete, it may be useful if the participants name the motives for their choice. This can be particularly meaningful for a play with a protagonist.

2. Clarification of needs

- Purpose: If there are different needs within a group these can be disclosed and a consensus or compromise can be found, allowing the group to function well together.

  Musical expression stimulates not only rational thoughts, but also feelings and preconscious impulses which can later be included in the analysis.

- Procedure: Each member selects an instrument and searches for an appropriate place on the stage, while walking and playing according to her mood related to the topic, expressing the topic musically.

  Then the scene is frozen. Each person briefly plays again and names her needs. The therapist names the goal, which is to find a group decision. Another period of playing follows. Subgroups may form.

  The scene is frozen again. Verbal possibilities can now come into play. The subgroups can now entice away members, or members can switch to a different subgroup. A serious, joyful play can emerge from a blocked situation, which builds energy for further work.

- Evaluation: Needs and opinions are exposed. If a group consensus cannot be reached, it is the responsibility of the therapist to promote compromise until all group members are again 'in the same boat'.

13 The "Social Atom" in Music Therapy

The social atom refers to the individual, and the roles and relationships in that individual's immediate social radius (Moreno 1959). It may be used in individual therapy as well as in groups. One can draw the social atom at the beginning and again at the end of therapy to show changes. This can enhance the awareness of the progress of the therapy and its transfer to life. The different parts of the social atom form a unit in our personality, a consonance of the roles, a role cluster.

13.1 The Social Atom in Individual Therapy

With the social atom one can view and analyze the innermost relationship landscape of a patient. In individual therapy, the patient is asked to choose an instrument, take it to the stage, and play on it. Then he is asked to choose an instrument for a person who is important to him and to set it down at an appropriate distance from the first instrument, and then play it, and so on, as long as very important persons keep coming to mind. The task of the therapist is to draw the set up, including the order of the choices for the symbolic persons and the manner of playing, so that it may be referred to in future sessions.

One may also draw the social atom (see Group Therapy) for subsequent discussion, with prominent personal relationships represented musically.

Steps in the adaptation process:

- As a rule, the patient first plays himself
- In the next step, the therapist imitates the patient on her instrument
- In the third step, the patient names the first important person, chooses an instrument for him or her, places it on the stage and plays the person
- In the fourth step, the patient and the therapist play together at the same time, or in a dialogue in which the patient plays himself and the therapist plays the important person
- Now the roles can be reversed
- Additional people from the social atom can be set up and duets performed

Since the instrument and not the therapist, symbolizes the role, the patient is never abandoned, even in difficult situations. If the therapist were to enact the psychodramatic roles, this could become problematic even if props are used as symbols; for example, if the therapist has to play an aggressive or possessive role with her body and voice. If she just plays an instrument, the threatening sound is still present and effective, yet the therapist remains available for the patient. This approach has also proven successful in therapy with children and is superior to psychodrama.

13.2 The Social Atom in Group Music Therapy

There are different therapeutic approaches for groups. One person can bring his social atom to the stage in a protagonist play, an approach similar to that used in individual therapy but with the difference that group members are chosen to play instruments set up on the stage for the different roles. It is also feasible for all the participants to draw their own social atoms and examine them together, after which some may enact theirs on stage.

Play modes for the social atom in group music therapy

1. The social atom as a protagonist play

At first glance the work resembles a "systemic constellation" from psychodrama. But the protagonist play goes further on three points: First, the participants are introduced to their roles and the protagonist remains the author. He may correct the participants: "Yes, this is the way it sounds!" "No, much louder and faster!" Second, the play approach by the protagonist is more individualistic than, for example, the family assembly/constellation. It addresses the inner representations of illness-causing, entrenched relationships and behavior patterns. Third, the social atom is a snapshot of an inner-relationship image for which the protagonist gets feedback from other group members, and which can be creatively affected by different forms of play.

- Purpose: To extend the self-image through the perception and feedback of the participants. Entrenched relationship patterns can be brought into motion with the play.

- Procedure: One group participant assembles the people closest to him on the stage with the help of the other participants. The protagonist chooses an instrument and a double – a person from the group who will play the protagonist's instrument when asked. Then he chooses an instrument for each personal relationship and a person to play it. He shows each player how to play, acting as composer and conductor; it is his play and composition!

  The therapist leads the play, suggests ways of playing, for instance, a duet for each relationship, role reversal in each relationship, or an ensemble play. The group also offers the possibility for the protagonist to sit in the spectator area and to listen to his relationship orchestra.

- Evaluation: Sharing and role feedback by the players, and the observations and identifications by the spectators are a treasure trove! This form of play is very valuable for personality development of the protagonist.

2. Drawing the social atom

- Purpose: By drawing the social atom, participants obtain a picture of the landscape of their current inner relationships. This picture alone can bring new insight. It may be used diagnostically or as a start for a protagonist play.

- Procedure: First, the group participants draw their own their social atoms, all at the same time. In this drawing they use symbols for male and female individuals. The degree of relatedness is represented by the distance on a line from the "I/ego" in the center. On this line, trouble in the relationship is marked by an "x". This process takes about 20 minutes.

- Evaluation: The drawings are examined by the group. The participants may ask questions about the drawings, although nobody has to comment on his own drawing. One may also cover up one's drawing. Later, some group members, together or one after the other, can bring their atom to the stage as a protagonist play with instruments and selected individuals from the group (see 1. The social atom as a protagonist play).

Figure 9. Students Analyze Social Atom Drawings with their Therapist

13.3 The Social Atom as a Diagnostic Tool

The social atom is a useful diagnostic tool in many areas, including child and adolescent psychiatry and geriatrics. It can reveal many problems affecting health – for example, traumatic relationships and losses, social imbalances of age, gender and environment, and problems with boundaries.

The suggestion to include important deceased persons can change the picture. The death of a person belonging to the social atom usually signifies the lasting effect of a loss. In work using the social atom, impairments of the relationship network caused by death, as well as current relationship dimensions, become visible. In general, the older the patient, the harder it is to adjust to losses.

Example from practice: drawing of an unusual social atom

The following drawing is by a member of an encounter group; it is the social atom of a 38-year-old married woman with three children. It is striking in that except for the partner, who is fully visible behind the woman, only female persons are represented in the drawing. The father is missing; the mother is far away with a line across the connection indicating a problem. The three children are very close; the sisters are fully cut off (the double lines separating them are very close to the patient). Two relatives (aunts) complete the picture. The drawing points to a serious problem; abuse cannot be excluded (the constellation of the close family, the problem with the relatives from the family of origin could be a clue).

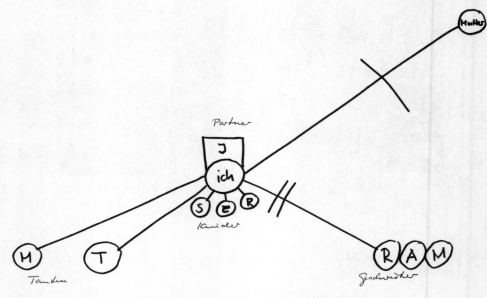

Figure 10. Drawing of an Unusual Social Atom by a 38-year old Woman

For her protagonist play she wants to limit herself to her current family. All four of them have to sit close to her and play their percussion instruments at the same rhythm. During role feedback she hears from the players that it was barely tolerable for the 'husband' and the 'children'. Then she begins to cry and says that her partner often does not come home anymore and possibly has a girlfriend. The drawing shows a problem (symbiosis), yet the protagonist did not draw a problem or any distance in the family, suggesting massive denial. I recommend psychotherapy for this woman because the work needed for her issues exceeds the possibilities offered in an encounter group.

Example from practice: social atom of a mother with a disabled daughter

Mrs. G is married and is the mother of two daughters. She suffers from exhaustion, depression and guilt feelings. Her social atom is striking.

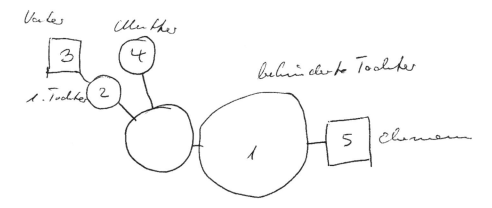

Figure 11. Social Atom of the Exhausted Mother of a Disabled Child

Mrs. G draws herself smaller than the disabled daughter who is in the center between her and her husband. Mrs. G explains that her husband takes part in the care of the younger daughter. Next to his job it is all he can do. The healthy older daughter is often looked after by her grandfather (father of the patient). Her mother also helps sometimes, but is already busy enough with her own household. The parents of the father (husband) live abroad; for other relationships there is no energy, time, nor desire.

In therapy, the music triggers sadness, anger, guilt feelings and exhaustion. A longer phase of emotional overload is followed by relaxation. She cries often and then feels relieved. After ten sessions she gets creative again and composes songs for the disabled daughter. A transfer occurs. She starts singing while giving care. The care-giving is less burdening and the child is becoming more cooperative, but despite this, Mrs. G. is in need of recuperation. With support from the pediatrician, her physician, her parents and her husband, it is made financially and physically possible for her to spend three weeks on vacation recovering, without her daughters. After this period she begins to be a bit more at peace with her fate, which is likely to remain a life-long task.

Process: At the beginning of therapy there was nothing "nourishing" in her environment. She learned to take better care of herself, to be a "good mother" to herself, too. The singing during the care improves the relationship with both the disabled and the healthy daughter, and improves her own well being. Taking care of herself also means looking for a cleaning service and getting assistance with the care-giving.

An "over-sized" part in the social atom may give an indication of a "bubble of feelings" from which feelings can flow in music therapy – in the above case sadness, anger, and guilt feelings. The "over-sized" disabled child also indicates an over-sized task for the couple. The social atom can also point to the type of help needed, and show what needs to be changed. This does not need to be therapy. Moreno (in: Leutz 1986) thinks it is often more effective to correct abnormalities in the social atom in practical ways, rather than to work on the physical and mental problems with therapy. When the relationships in the social atom are not supportive of the protagonist, one has to evaluate which ones exceed the realm of therapy. One should encourage patients to seek additional help and take further steps to, for instance, move to a different environment, find new friends, consider foster care for the children, move to a different place, move back, change jobs, divorce, etc.

14 The Cultural Atom

The cultural atom is a further development of the social atom and concerns our cultural roles, such as neighbor, community member, citizen, professional, occupant of a nursing home. It deals with our transcendent roles, not with the clarification of relationships with individuals such as a certain neighbor, friend, partner or colleague, but with inner representations of our own cultural share. When musical instruments are used as symbols, it becomes apparent which cultural roles are pleasing and fulfilling for the patients, where their lives are meaningful and enjoyable, where they are over- or underchallenged, and what erodes and drains their energy. In this area, too, concrete assistance in addition to therapy or instead of therapy can make sense.

Example from practice: Cultural atom of a music therapy student

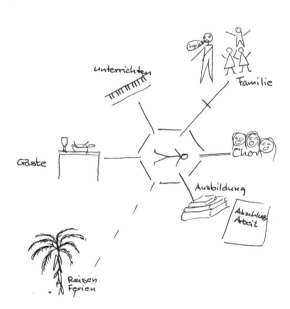

Figure 12. The Cultural Atom of a Music Therapy Student.

This 40-year-old student became aware of her real stress from this drawing. In the musical implementation, her perfectionism also became apparent. She learned to 'pin her ideals to the stars' where they belong, where they may serve as guidance on life's journey; and to strive for the achievable on earth, setting priorities, which is work on the transcendental level.

The cultural atom can be a guidepost to new meaning in life. It can help with coming to terms with multiple exceptional talents. The musical play representing the cultural atom can show which roles the patient no longer wants, which ones are desired, and which ones need changing. The music quickly makes audible which roles are too demanding. This "cultural orchestra" may be changed; the same instrument may be played in different ways. In this manner, health-damaging patterns of cultural roles and one-sidedness, such as isolation and a life bereft of content/meaning can be exposed.

Example from practice of a cultural atom: a patient with burnout syndrome

The patient is 57 years old. He was declared ill by the psychiatrist and was referred to individual therapy because he collapsed at work.

He draws his cultural atom; his most important roles are director and president of a company. Whenever he undertakes something, he is the leader. Partnerships fail.

He chooses a trumpet for himself and drums for the other roles. After playing his roles, he sits down, tired. "I miss the cello, but I don't know how to play it. Only drums and the trumpet! I would like to be able to follow along, not lead" he concludes.

In the next therapy phase he develops his ability of going along, playing along, and relinquishing the lead. He becomes aware of his fear of loss of control. He learns to discern themes and rhythms, to adapt them and also to tolerate chaos. He recovers, can sleep again, and builds a new partnership. With the help of the firm's social worker he changes his work area and his tasks in the organization.

Example from practice: the cultural atom of a patient with depressive disorder

The opposite of the previous case is seen in the cultural atom of a 47-year-old woman with depressive moods. Her cultural roles have two things in common: serving and waiting! Waiting for the children to come home from school, for the husband to come home, for customers to come to the store and to know what they want. This woman likes these roles quite well, as she says. She is mother, wife, sales person, and yet she feels unhappy. It is thus a matter of having to examine the cultural roles more closely.

As she examines the assembly of instruments for her cultural atom, the monochord, chimes (metal tubes with lasting resonance, hanging on strings) and a metallophone, she says: "I need a rhythm, one which I can determine myself." She picks the djembe. She practices "self-assertion", alone and next to others. She learns to notice her impulses, acknowledge them, and express them. Her depressed mood disappears within a short time. In the existing roles of mother, wife, and sales person she changes the part of "waiting", becomes more active and more self-asserting. She ends the therapy and wants to venture into a creative hobby with other women.

Process: Work with the social atom brought role transparency which made it easier for the patient to break away from her role fixations and to consciously try to make changes.

In individual therapy or counseling, the patient chooses an instrument to represent the "self" as well as one for each role to be played. In a group, one may also choose a person to play an instrument for each activity. This makes it possible to hear how the inner orchestra sounds. It becomes apparent what changes offer themselves up or impose themselves.

Another way of making internalized roles transparent is to personify thoughts, feelings and strengths, etc. This encompasses all of the following: the rejecting, strong, fearful, pessimistic person; the Pollyanna, the conservative, the conceited person, the noble lady, the inner therapist, the strict teacher, the inner baby, etc. One assigns them an instrument and gives them a musical voice. Music is always emotional, but never moralistic. It helps to mold the personified inner voices and forces in an emotional way without reflection. Through role assignment, the music becomes comprehensible. The sounds and the experiences can be labeled in relation to the roles and can be varied musically in the next scene, until the inner orchestra suits the protagonist, who is the composer as well as the conductor.

Play modes for the cultural atom in music therapy

Transcendental roles are at the center of the cultural atom. The focus is inner balance, new orientation, life perspectives, community, country, and integration of losses. Rituals may be helpful (see Transcendental Warm-Up). Here I would like to point to other possibilities:

1. Perspectives play

- Purpose: To develop individual perspectives through playing, to expand possibilities, and to sort out unrealizable dreams (as idea reserves, fantasies, expectations of others, etc.).

- Procedure: We start by planning scenes for the topic "The cultural roles I have today and may have in 5, 10 or 20 years". The protagonist selects an instrument for herself and chooses a double. Then she stages her current cultural atom (partnership, job situation, family, children, living situation, etc.), each with an instrument and a performer who gets instructions on how to play. Once the scene is set up, the protagonist sits in the center and plays her instrument or listens to the orchestra. Then she decides what to bring to the next stage/station of life, what to leave behind and what to add. At the new station, new musical movements with different ways of playing or new constellations are possible.

- Evaluation: Sharing/feedback round.

2. The "culture orchestra"

- Purpose: To develop identity and self-image as well as appearance. Expand self knowledge, promote feelings of self worth, improve familiarity in the group.

- Procedure: The cultural atom can first be drawn in a group. Participants can present their own "culture orchestra" to the group. For each role, with a limit of four central roles, an instrument and player are set up on stage. The players are given instructions about the improvisation. They may also be directed by the protagonist.

- Evaluation: Feedback from the spectators and role players.

3. "Group identity"

- Purpose: To bring out transcendental commonalities and differences in a group. This mode of play can also aid team development.

- Procedure: Group members draw the topics individually, for example, about their professional identity, or their identity as a politician, or member of a team. The drawings are discussed together. Each member can present an important component of his cultural atom with an instrument on stage. In this manner a "professions orchestra", a "politicians' orchestra", or a "team orchestra" is created. Differences may come to the center of attention.

- Evaluation: Sharing/feedback round, possibly followed by formulating universally valid identity characteristics which were noted.

15 Processing

Processing or process analysis is done by the patients, if need be with therapeutic assistance, in group as well as individual therapy. Questions (who did what, where, how, when) are examined together and presented. The goal is to remember the process and be conscious of it, allowing the often fleeting emotional experiences in music therapy to be held on to. As a consequence, newly gained insights are not only named, but are relived emotionally and represented with symbols. Thus, a replay in a different medium takes place, providing better integration of events into one's awareness and improving sustainability. A time interval between the observed process and its analysis is helpful; the events can settle in, and the recalled memory with the distance in time enhances the sustainability (Besser 2004).

With processing, connections become visible. In particular, the connection from the group process to one's own issues usually becomes very clear as group members discover how their play helps others or how they get pushed by others in their own process. The therapists have another opportunity here to point out the important progress made by the participants. This process in individual therapy is not significantly different from the work in groups. The patient also establishes his "therapy path", traces once more the different stations, and symbolically collects the valuable things found along the way. Processing is also "harvesting".

15.1 The Process Assembly

One way to process is the process assembly; in this approach the common path is spatially represented with musical instruments and other symbols. Each instrument in the assembly can be replayed, and each station can be named again verbally. The therapist who is in possession of notes for the process analysis makes sure that no important experiences or changes are left out. Brief feedback enforces sustainability. Often, a photograph of the processing set-up marks the end of a therapy and leads into the concluding farewells.

Example from practice from an encounter course with music therapists

The following play is from a 2 ½-day encounter course. The 14 participants are music therapists with various educational backgrounds.

We start with the processing 1 ½hours before parting. After the last play, the stage is cleared, followed by a break. Now, we recall the entire process together. How did we start? The therapist uses her notes. Many of the participants have also written in their diaries. Each person presents his or her most special experience and chooses symbols, usually musical instruments, sometimes personal objects or mementos, and explains what he or she wants to express with them. We go through the sequence once more, step by step. By observing the same timing of the events, the steps of each participant are presented in connection with the steps of the other participants. This provides an overview of the effects, from one therapy step to the next.

*Figure 13. Group Participants Analyze the Process Together and Place Symbols
for Each Important Event on the Process Path.*

The re-living together of crucial remembered moments provides an overview which can
be examined from different viewpoints and then evaluated. The participants assess which
plays of their predecessors moved them, where they were able to identify, where their own
issues came into motion so strongly that they were able to bring them to the stage, the effects of warming up on the group, etc. From the process path, they visually recognize how
each event developed from the previous one. What is experienced is that many emotions are
named for the first time. A plentiful harvest! We photograph the process path to give the
participants a souvenir picture so they can look at it again later and remember the process,
then we transition to goodbyes.

During processing it consistently becomes clear that the play by the protagonist
has resonance in the group and influences the course of the process. In the group
process, connections become transparent. If the path of the process is captured by
a picture which is given to the participants, the lasting effect of the group experience and the energy available is enhanced. Pictures are superior to notes (according
to surveys of participants). Instead of the process path, the image of a stream may
be used as a symbol for the process.

With processing, not only the issues, but also the mental states of the participants, their contentment, and sometimes their problems in getting along with other
participants, become clear. If so, the therapist has the opportunity to address these
during the farewell round.

15.2 The Process Drawing

An additional form of process analysis can be a drawing, as seen in the following illustration which was done at the end of a therapy with an adolescent.

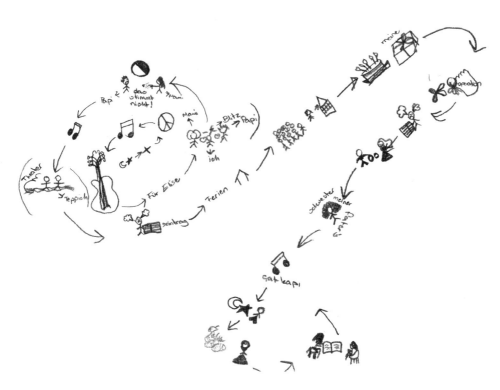

Figure 14. Process Drawing (pencil, 1:1) by a 14-year-old Adolescent after Two Years of Therapy.

Together with the therapist, who has reflected in advance on the process and brings her notes to the processing session, the patient recalls steps and events important to him and draws them. For each step a symbol is used, creating a personal, individually drawn picture of the common path. The therapist mentions events which she deems important and the patient decides whether or not to include them in his drawing. These pictures are usually so encoded that uninformed observers cannot decipher them.

The drawing is a creative product, often a small piece of art which may be put into a diary or hung on the wall, to look at it over and over again. Children and adolescents often tell me when I happen to see them, "I still have the drawing!" Through repeated recall, the effect is sustained and the transfer energy is strengthened (Besser 2004).

16 Music Therapy and Psychodrama: A Productive Pair

Music therapy and psychodrama are both valuable methods. With combined forces, like a well-functioning couple, they achieve even more together. They are a good match. The foundations of music therapy and psychodrama have similarities with respect to resonance, spontaneity, and creativity. The fact that improvisation – the spontaneous, creative, and playful answer to the unforeseen – is so central to both methods, is a key reason that most structural psychodrama elements can be well integrated into music therapy. As shown in the examples from practice, the spectrum of effects may be broadened by combining the two methods. I would like to emphasize the following aspects of this point:

Strengthening musical events: Assembly of assigned musical instruments on the stage is the first conscious, creative, self-determined action relating to the topic. The therapist is the assistant director and makes sure that the patient takes enough time and space for the staging. Thus the musical play which will lead into the depths of emotions is first experienced in a deeply self-determined way. Improvisations, which are approached differently, also include self-determination, but it is often not experienced as strongly. The experience of self-determination helps develop a sense of self-effectiveness, the sense of being able to influence one's own life. This notion facilitates changes and learning, as neurological research demonstrates (Spitzer 2005).

Enhanced access to suffering: Sociometric interventions can support music therapeutic diagnostics. Targeted warming up provides patients with the necessary energy to handle their suffering creatively.

Bridges between the unconscious and the conscious: Psychodrama elements such as scene setting, role reversal, sharing, and feedback offer excellent opportunities to bridge the unconscious with the conscious without interpretation.

Roles as access to resources: By dissecting a role cluster and breaking down a situation into different participants, detailed sorting of inner strengths, or presenting of a problematic situation with different roles, healthy components can be recognized, grasped, and readily applied in the setting-up of instruments.

The emerging role-transparency can facilitate the release from fixations. Likewise, dysfunctional components can be recognized by role assignments and worked on with musical play.

Support and immersion through session structure: The three-act structure (targeted warming up, play with scene setting and role assignments, sharing and feedback) can provide stability for the patient and deepen the process. The targeted warming up stimulates energy and memories. Creation of a mental image (the patient is asked to allow a mental picture to emerge and to remember a corresponding episode from his past) further stimulates awareness. Role assignment is a conscious act during scene building. The positions of the individual roles in the whole role framework are spatially organized. This first creative job brings focus and support to the process. The conscious process of shaping the scenes, acting causatively in the experience brings security. The musical improvisation that follows deepens the experience emotionally; it is open and largely uncontrollable. Crucial mental processes occur at this point. In the third step, the verbal sharing and feedback round, these experiences are put into words. This part brings focus, and through verbalization (preferably without interpretation), brings the process into the present consciousness. This connects the musical event more closely to the process.

Transfer and sustainability: These gentle, transparent psychodrama elements are valuable additions to the volatile music therapy, and are clearly better remembered in connection with the individual process than straight music therapeutic interventions. In listening to audio recordings with patients, it is striking that the patients, as well as the therapist, immediately remember therapy situations, even when only short excerpts are played. This intense recall of a situation when listening hardly ever happens with straight music therapy improvisations. Often, it is no longer clear who played what. As soon as role assignments come into play, these are immediately remembered. The musical events are obviously better retained in connection with psychodramatic elements. Neurology research confirms that the more brain areas are active during a learning step, the better it is remembered (Spitzer 2002). Multi-leveled memory tracks are created by:

- Demands on the patient's imagination when getting started on the topic
- Clearly stated meaning attributed to instruments, and the role assignments and forms of music played
- Visualization during scene setting
- Verbal reconstruction after the play (sharing/feedback)
- Processing (symbolic representation of the process path)

This enables the process to be comprehensible and recallable, thus facilitating the transfer of changes which were acquired in therapy, to daily life.

More transfer of dissociated or repressed parts to therapy: Scene setting and feedback are gentle approaches to let the patient know that the therapist also appreciates the repressed parts, finds them important, and includes them. The patient remains free to decide what to do with them.

More transfer from therapy to daily life: The process can be supported with feedback, work on perspectives, and processing and contracts (concrete agreements with patients), Psychodrama elements in music therapy stand out for their strong transfer capacity.

List of Tables and Figures

Tables

Figures

Bibliography

Ameln, F. v., Gerstmann, R. & Kramer, J. (2009). Psychodrama. 2. Auflage Berlin, Heidelberg: Springer

Anzieu, D. (1984). Analytisches Psychodrama mit Kindern und Jugendlichen. Paderborn: Junfermann

Bauer, J. (2006). Warum ich fühle, was du fühlst, Intuitive Kommunikation und das Geheimnis der Spiegelneurone. München: Heine

Belliger, A. u. Krieger, D. J. (2003). Ritualtheorien. Wiesbaden: Westdeutscher Verlag

Besser, R. (2004). Transfer: Damit Seminare Früchte tragen, Strategien, Übungen und Methoden, die eine konkrete Umsetzung in die Praxis sichern. Weinheim und Basel: Beltz

Burmeister, J. (1997). Diagnostik im therapeutischen Psychodrama. Script, unveröffentlicht

Burmeister, J. (2004). Diagnostik im therapeutischen Psychodrama. In: Fürst, J. Ottomeyer, K. & Pruckner, H. (Hrsg.). Psychodramatherapie, ein Handbuch. Wien: Facultas. 81–102

Decker-Voigt, H. H. (Hrsg.) (2001). Schulen der Musiktherapie. München: Reinhardt

Dettmer, B. (2004). Die Familienskulptur und ihre Variationen in der Musiktherapie. In: Zeuch A., Hänsel, M. & Jungaberle, H. Systemische Konzepte für die Musiktherapie. Heidelberg: Carl-Auer Systeme. 90–110

Dieckmann, H. (1991). Komplexe, Diagnostik und Therapie in der Analytischen Psychologie, Berlin/ Heidelberg: Springer

Dobberstein, M. (2000). Musik und Mensch, Grundlegung einer Anthropologie der Musik. Berlin: Reimer

Fausch, H. (1989). Ästhetik und die Destruktivität der Ideale, Magazin Primarschule 2/89. 29–33

Frohne-Hagemann, I. (1993). Musiktherapeutische Diagnostik und Manual nach ICD 10. Göttingen: Vandenhoeck & Ruprecht

Frohne-Hagemann, I. (2001). Fenster zur Musiktherapie, Musik-therapie-theorie 1976–2001. Wiesbaden: zeitpunkt musik, Reichert

Frohne-Hagemann, I. (2005). Indikation Musiktherapie bei psychischen Problemen im Jugendalter. Göttingen: Vandenhoeck & Ruprecht

Frohne-Hagemann, I. (1997). Die heilende Beziehung als therapeutisches Medium und ihre musiktherapeutische Gestaltung. In: Müller, L. & Petzold, H. G. (Hrsg.). Musiktherapie in der klinischen Arbeit. Integrative Modelle und Methoden. Praxis der Musiktherapie. Band 16. Stuttgart: Gustav Fischer. 9–22

Gindl, B. (2002). Anklang, Die Resonanz der Seele. Paderborn: Junferman

Guth, H. (2005). Musiktherapeutische Ansätze mit hörgeschädigten Kindern. In: Tüpker, R., Hippel, N. & Laabs, F. (Hrsg.). Musiktherapie in der Schule. Wiesbaden: zeitpunkt musik, Reichert. 137–158

Hegi, F. (1998). Übergänge zwischen Sprache und Musik, Die Wirkungskomponenten der Musiktherapie. Paderborn: Junfermann

Hegi, F. (2010). Improvisation und Musiktherapie, Möglichkeiten und Wirkungen von frei-
er Musik. Wiesbaden: zeitpunkt musik, Reichert

Hegi-Portmann, F., Lutz Hochreutener, S. & Rüdisüli-Voerkel, M. (2006). Musiktherapie
als Wissenschaft, Grundlagen, Praxis, Forschung und Ausbildung. Zürich

Hegi, F., Rüdisüli M. (2011). Der Wirkung von Musik auf der Spur. Wiesbaden: zeitpunkt
musik, Reichert

Heidegger, M. (2004). Gesamtausgabe, 4. Abteilung, Hinweise und Aufzeichnungen, Band
87 Nietzsche Seminare 1937 u. 1944: Frankfurt am Main, Vittorio Klostermann. 294

Hofer-Werner, G. (1998). Die Bedeutung von Musik in Mythen und Märchen. Bern:
Schriften über Harmonik Nr. 23.

Hüther, G. (2004). Ebenen salutogenetischer Wirkungen von Musik auf das Gehirn. In:
Musiktherapeutische Umschau, 25 (1), Göttingen: Vandenhoeck & Ruprecht. 16–25

Jungaberle, H. (2004). Musiktherapie – systemisch, polyzentrisch, polyphon. In: Zeuch,
A., Hänsel, M. & Jungaberle H. (Hrsg.). Systemische Konzepte für die Musiktherapie.
Heidelberg: Carl-Auer Systeme. 13–31

Krüger, R. (1989). Der Rollentausch und seine tiefenpsychologische Funktion. Sonder-
druck, Artikel für die Zeitschrift Psychodrama

Krüger, R. (1997). Kreative Interaktion, tiefenpsychologische Theorie und Methoden des
klassischen Psychodramas. Göttingen: Vandenhoeck & Ruprecht

Lammers, K. (2004). Allgemeine Techniken im Psychodrama. In: Fürst, J., Ottomeyer, K.
& Pruckner, H. (Hrsg.). Psychodramatherapie, ein Handbuch. Wien: Facultas. 222–243

Leutz, G. (1986). Psychodrama, das klassische Psychodrama nach Moreno. Berlin/ Heidelberg: Springer

Lowen, A. (1991). Körper, Ausdruck und Persönlichkeit. München: Kösel

Lutz Hochreutener, S. (2009). Spiel – Musik – Therapie, Methoden der Musiktherapie mit
Kindern und Jugendlichen. Göttingen: Hogrefe

Mentzos, St. (19849). Neurotische Konfliktverarbeitung. Frankfurt am Main: Fischer

Moreno, J. J. (1999). Acting your inner Music. Saint Louis: MMB, Inc.

Moreno, J. L. (1981). Soziometrie als experimentelle Methode. Paderborn: Junfermann

Müller, L. (1997). Integrative Musiktherapie in der Behandlung eines Kindes mit schwerer,
früher Entwicklungs- und Persönlichkeitsstörung. In: Müller, L. & Petzold, H. G.
(Hrsg.). Musiktherapie in der klinischen Arbeit. Integrative Modelle und Methoden.
Praxis der Musiktherapie. Band 16. Stuttgart: Gustav Fischer. 137–167

Müller L. & Petzold, H. G. (Hrsg.) (1997). Musiktherapie in der klinischen Arbeit. Integrative
Modelle und Methoden. Praxis der Musiktherapie. Band 16. Stuttgart: Gustav Fischer

Nöcker-Ribaupierre, M. (1995). Auditive Stimulation nach Frühgeburt. Ein Beitrag zur
Musiktherapie. Stuttgart: Gustav Fischer

Oeltze, H.-J. (1997). Intermediale Arbeit in der Integrativen Musiktherapie. In: Müller, L. &
Petzold, H. G. (Hrsg.). Musiktherapie in der klinischen Arbeit. Integrative Modelle und
Methoden. Praxis der Musiktherapie. Band 16. Stuttgart: Gustav Fischer Verlag. 113–136

Papoušek, M. (1994). Vom ersten Schrei zum ersten Wort. Bern: Huber

Piontelli, A. (1996). Vom Fetus zum Kind: Die Ursprünge des psychischen Lebens. Eine psychoanalytische Beobachtungsstudie. Stuttgart: Klett-Cotta

Plahl, Ch. und Koch-Temming, H. (2005). Musiktherapie mit Kindern, Grundlagen, Methoden, Praxisfelder. Bern: Hans Huber

Sartre, J.-P. (1997). Die Transzendenz des Ego. Philosophische Essays (1931–1939). Berlin: Rowohlt

Schacht, M. (2004). Entwicklungstheoretische Skizzen. In: Fürst, J., Ottomeyer, K. & Pruckner, H. (Hrsg.). Psychodramatherapie, ein Handbuch. Wien: Facultas. 104–127

Schmölz, A. (1983). Zum Begriff der Einstimmung in der Musiktherapie. In: Decker-Voigt, H. H. (Hrsg.). Handbuch der Musiktherapie. Lilienthal/Bremen: Eres

Schumacher, K. (1994). Musiktherapie mit autistischen Kindern. Praxis der Musiktherapie Band 12. Stuttgart: Fischer

Schumacher, K., Calvet-Kruppa, C. (1999). Musiktherapie als Weg zum Spracherwerb. Musiktherapeutische Umschau. Band 20 (3), Göttingen: Vandenhoeck & Ruprecht. 216–230

Schumacher, K., Calvet, C. (2007). Synchronisation, Musiktherapie bei Kindern mit Autismus. Göttingen: Vandenhoeck & Ruprecht

Spitzer, M. (2003). Musik im Kopf, Hören, Musizieren, Verstehen und Erleben im neuronalen Netzwerk. Stuttgart: Schattauer

Spitzer, M. (2002). Lernen: Gehirnforschung und Schule des Lebens. Heidelberg: Spektrum, Akad. Verlag

Spitzer, M. (2004). Selbstbestimmen, Gehirnforschung und die Frage, was sollen wir tun? München: Elsevier (Spektrum, Akad. Verlag)

Springer, R. (1995). Grundlagen einer Psychodramapädagogik. Köln: inScenario

Stern, D. N. (2007). Die Lebenserfahrung des Säuglings. Stuttgart: Klett Cotta

Timmermann, T. (2003). Klingende Systeme, Aufstellungsarbeit und Musiktherapie. Heidelberg: Carl-Auer Systeme

Timmermann, T. (2004). Tiefenpsychologisch orientierte Musiktherapie. Bausteine für eine Lehre. Wiesbaden: Reichert

Tüpker, R., Hippel, N. & Laabs, F. (2005). Musiktherapie in der Schule. Wiesbaden: zeitpunkt musik, Reichert

Wieser M. (2004). Wirksamkeitsnachweise für die Psychodrama-Therapie. In: Fürst, J., Ottomeyer, K. & Pruckner, H. (Hrsg.). Psychodramatherapie, ein Handbuch. Wien: Facultas. 427–446

Winnicott, D. W. (1985). Vom Spiel zur Kreativität. Stuttgart: Klett Cotta

Zeuch, A., Hänsel, M. & Jungaberle, H. (2004). Systemische Konzepte für die Musiktherapie. Heidelberg: Carl-Auer Systeme

English Bibliography

Note: the English translation of the original "Musiktherapie und Psychodrama" contains quotes which were taken from the German references listed above. Below are references written in English on the same subjects.

Baim, C., Burmeister, J., Maciel, M. (2007). Psychodrama: Advances in Theory and Practice. USA: Taylor and Frances.

Frohne-Hagemann, I. (2004). Receptive Music Therapy: Theory and Practice. Forum Zeitpunkt: Zeitpunkt Musik.

Gershoni, J. (ed.) (2003). Psychodrama in the 21st Century. Clinical and Educational Applications. New York: Springer Publishing Company.

Gessmann, H.-W. (1994). Humanistic Psychodrama. Vol. I–IV. Duisburg, Germany: PIB Publisher.

Kapp, M., Holmes, P., Bradshaw Tauvon, K. (eds.) (1998). The Handbook of Psychodrama. New York/ London: Routledge.

Landy, R. J. (2007). The Couch and the Stage: Integrating Words and Action in Psychotherapy. New York: Jason Aronson.

Moreno, J. J. (1999). Acting your inner Music. Saint Louis: MMB, Inc.

Nordoff, P. and Robbins, C. (1977). Creative Music Therapy. New York: John Day & Co. [out of print].

Nordoff, P. and Robbins, C. (2007). Creative Music Therapy: a Guide to fostering Clinical Musicianship. 2nd ed., revised. Gilsum, N. H.: Barcelona Publishers.

Smeijsters, H. (2005). Sounding the Self: Analogy in improvisational Music Therapy. Gilsum, N. H.: Barcelona Publishers.

Stern, D. N. (2000). The Interpersonal World Of The Infant. A View From Psychoanalysis And Developmental Psychology. New York: Basic Books.

Yablonsky, L. (1981). Psychodrama: Resolving Emotional Problems through Role-playing. New York: Gardner, 1981.

Winnicott, D. W. (2005). Playing and Reality. New York: Routledge Classics. Routledge, Taylor & Francis Group.

Index

security 15, 16, 41, 45, 50, 62, 77–79, 83, 86, 89, 93, 100,104, 142

self-acceptance 110,

self-awareness 16, 17, 25, 45, 59, 70, 79, 80, 92

sharing 29 (definition), 35, 45, 57, 141

social atom 19, 25, 29, 125–131, 133

sociometry 11, 21, 28, 30, 31, 56, 83, 119–122

songs 12, 13, 28, 86, 130

soothe 83

sound 13–19, 27, 56, 59, 60, 71, 76, 78, 83, 86, 88, 92, 97, 117, 127

spectator 28–30, 80, 86, 93, 103, 105, 123, 128

spirituality 21, 38, 83, 92

spontaneity 19, 21, 30, 33, 37, 41, 42, 70, 141

stage in psychodrama 28

stories 18, 27, 34, 76, 98

structure 11, 13, 31, 32, 34, 55, 64, 87, 88, 111, 120, 141

supervision 11, 21, 33, 64, 67, 81, 84, 109

symbol 11,14, 16, 39, 47, 50, 52, 56, 81, 83, 84, 90, 98, 127, 129, 133, 137,138

synchronization 17, 24, 36 38, 40, 116

system 11, 15, 17, 20, 22, 33, 35, 58, 95

systemic 19–21, 28, 97, 128,

T

targeted warm up 92

tele 20–24, 33, 35–39

tele relationship 22–24

therapeutic function 95

touched, touching 37, 47, 60, 74, 76, 85, 90, 100

transcendence, transcendental 25–27, 31, 69, 83–86, 91, 133, 135, 136

transfer 11, 39, 40, 44, 45 53, 62, 100, 102, 105, 127, 132, 139, 142

transference 23–24, 37, 58, 92, 101, 105

transition 44, 57, 88, 93, 94, 138

tuning, tune in, join in 16, 34, 56, 69, 86,

V

verbalize, verbalization 62, 63, 142

voice 46, 48, 52, 60, 63, 73, 74, 80, 85, 86, 90, 92, 127, 135